Tha...
Carlos!!

DEREK AGONS
SLAYS A DRAGON

♡ 4 EVER ♡

SAMUEL TUCKER YOUNG

DEDICATION

To my friends and my family, you know I could not do
this without you.

Especially you, Mom and Dad.

CONTENTS

ACKNOWLEDGMENTS

Sonni, seriously, thank you for listening to me as I rambled on for years about this silly little universe. The need to impress you has driven me to absolute insanity, but it has also driven me to make this real.

PROLOGUE

"It doesn't seem like a dragon's lair," the man named Prometheus mused, licking his lips in contempt. "It looks more like a common old cave; dank and not worth a piss." He scratched the long and flowing white beard that clung to his high cheekbones, observing the mountain before him. After a few moments, he repeated the words under his breath and began to chuckle at his own wit. Indeed, Prometheus seemed to do that a lot. For whatever reason, he always found himself the most amusing creature amongst the colleagues of his own race.

The cat would never understand how Prometheus could think such a preposterous thought. A very, very, long time ago, Prometheus must have been a brilliant mind. Why else would he have been so well renowned by his own race? The great professor Randall Prometheus's name carried weight as an excellent explorer in a world with no secrets. It was, in fact, why the cat had sought the man's company in the first place, regardless of the consequences of his own kind. Sure, letting any single human know of the cat's very existence was forbidden, but this continuing age of humans was growing more and more dull by the second. The cat had thought that, together, he and Prometheus could discover the last great curiosity that the world held.

Of course, that was before the cat had heard the professor open his mouth. The cat breathed deeply, letting the grating sound of the man's voice wash over him. In truth, Prometheus was easily the least amusing creature he had ever encountered. "Rest assured, Prometheus," the cat began coolly, stretching his velvet back and hopping onto the rock the old and gangly man sat upon. "When I throw around a phrase such as 'dragon's lair,' I mean it." The cat sniffed the air, tasting for any hint of danger. His golden eyes were locked on the cave opening in front of them. "It's not a very common occurrence."

"Fine, *cat*," Prometheus spat, squatting down on the boulder. He crossed his arms in contempt. Together, they overlooked the clearing before them. It was a peaceful little glade, completely unassuming and outwardly worthless, though it carried with it an unbridled feeling of a lost age. The grass was shin high and golden to the eye, swaying gently and ever glistening against the glow of the sun. The trees that surrounded it were old and burdened with time, each massive in size and weight. Their trunks stretched wide, their leaves hung low, and even their bark was riddled with deep and countless ridges from side to side. None of these parts could match their summation, though. The cat let the chills run down his spine, lavishing in their presence, as he let his breathing match the wind. He stared forward, his tail swaying and ready. At the edge of the clearing, beyond the tree trunks and shimmering blades of grass, sat the base of a lonely little mountain and its singular yet modest opening.

"Just as long as this book you've talked so much about is inside," Prometheus said, breaking the cat's concentration. The cat could barely hide his contempt, but Prometheus did not notice. There were a great many things that the man named Prometheus did not seem to notice. "I don't care what it is," Prometheus continued with a scoff. "It can be a dragon's cave or hide a bunch of kittens, or a nest of bananas! Just get on with it already—"

Instantly, the cave opening burst into flames, sending Prometheus reeling to the ground in terror. However, it was not from the sight of the majestic blaze, nor was it the earth rattling underfoot as the beast finally stirred from within. No, the cat mused, it must have been the sound itself that sent Prometheus into an absolute panic. The roar had been thick and dripping with times long past. It had been said long ago that a dragon's laugh could melt the heaviest mind. How much more so could its roar tear apart the faintest of hearts? The cat cleansed himself in the sound, reveling in its majesty. The feline did not realize how much he had missed it. Its reverberations were as old as the mountains and as deafening as the sea, a roar that could crush bones.

The cat watched the flames burst into smoke and ash with a smile. The smoke began to swirl like a hurricane, compressing at its very center, until eventually the cave's opening exploded in a gigantic blur of motion that erupted directly into the sky. The dragon shot upward with the ease of a swan, twirling and unfolding his massive wings. Prometheus cowered under the dragon's shadow, hoping his shivering would be enough to hide him. Another roar escaped the beast's jaws, shaking the surrounding clouds from their seldom-bothered perches. The dragon hovered for a brief instant, surveying the area around it, before giving off another roar and blasting off into the horizon.

The cat tried to smile, but could not. Sometimes, the plans set in place happen so perfectly it almost stopped being fun.

"What the hell just happened?" Prometheus yelled at the top of a whisper, crawling forward on his hands and knees. He kept a wary eye on the sky, cowering at even the slightest breeze. He brought himself to his knees and brushed off his once subdued yellow khakis, foolishly trying to restore some hint of the gleam they once carried.

"Where did the bloody beast scurry off to?" He adjusted the satchel on his shoulder, worriedly.

The cat hopped off the rock without a second thought or answer. Quickly, for even he did not look forward to coming toe to toe with a dragon, he crossed the little clearing. The cat did not wait for Prometheus as he made his way to the now smoldering cave opening. "Most likely the beast, as you so plainly called it, simply left," the cat called casually over his shoulder. "He probably went off in search for his egg after he realized the one he was sitting on was no more than a perfectly round and heated rock that I may or may not have switched it with last night while the pair of you were asleep." The cat licked his lips in pleasure, allowing himself a small breath. The only thing better than a well thought out plan was the incredibly long sentence that followed it.

"The dragon has an egg?" Prometheus wondered aloud. He picked up his pace and followed the cat into the mouth of the cave. His words bounced against the walls of the mountain, reverberating loudly enough for the world to hear. The cat's eyes shook in anguish. The poor feline could scarce keep from getting a headache when Prometheus spoke at a normal level, much less an amplified one. "What did you do?" Prometheus continued his questioning, trying to keep in step. His poor human eyes were not as well adjusted to the darkened corridors inside the mountain. "Did you destroy it?" The cat could hear Prometheus's heart race with each step. They were venturing further and further into the earth now, down to where no creature has set foot in ages. The cat felt his own heart pick up at the thought.

"Don't be ridiculous," he scoffed at Prometheus's words. "The dragon's egg is protected with a darker knowledge than even I know." His tail began to flick back and forth as he processed the thought. "I just made it appear missing. The beast will figure the trick out soon enough."

The inside of the cave was absolutely massive. Prometheus could not tell if it was properly a cave anymore, seeing how far down into the mountain they had walked. In fact, the dragon's lair was more of an underground grotto. Stalactites reached across the surface in every direction, descending directly to the grotto's floor. Prometheus felt his mind racing. This is what he lived for, what he had always dreamed of. He had just set foot into a world no man had ever seen, that no man could even fathom. This was a thing of fairytales and storybooks! He knew as he looked around that he had found his discerning moment, that he was looking at what would be his greatest discovery. He was in a dragon's lair.

It was surprisingly clean, as far as dragon's lairs went, not that Prometheus knew of any. He had always thought of dragons as oversized pack rats with wings, but it seemed he had it all wrong. This dragon in particular was far cleverer, far more organized. Odd trinkets ranging from armor to other ancient necessities were stacked a mile high as far the eye could see, but the piles themselves seemed to be in some sort of order. Prometheus could not figure it out for the life of him, though he could feel the pattern's existence. He shook off the thought, keeping his mind clean for what really mattered. He was not here for trinkets from faded ages. He was here for the greatest treasure of them all.

Prometheus knew it when he saw it. There, in the middle of the cavern, sat a central mound of boulders. They were peculiarly placed, even at first glance. Each was piled high in an almost step stone formation, though they were steps clearly made for a beast as big as a dragon. Prometheus sprinted for it, his pulse pounding in his ears. It took longer than he would have liked and the strength of his entire body to climb just one step, but eventually he made his way to the top. The boulders gave way to a large crater in the middle of the cave, fashioned in such a way that he assumed it could only be the dragon's bed. The stones here were much smoother, more round, more perfectly placed. He searched frantically with his eyes, crawling over stone and stone alike. He made his way to the center of the bed, hoping for what he would find. No, he stopped the thought in its tracks. He knew what he would find. He knew what he would finally have in his grasp.

"Here it is!" he shrieked. He should have thought twice about lifting his voice, but he could not help it. He reached down and removed a strange, yellow tinted rock in the exact middle of the boulders. Beneath it sat a lone book, older than the first heartbeat. Prometheus did not even have time to notice the perfectly egg-shaped rock that had been split in two.

"Cat, I found it!" he shouted, wrapping up the old text in his arms. The book was older than old; it defied the very definition. Its pages were frayed and its cover was tattered, yet it did not smell or hint of deterioration. Instead, there it sat, perfectly ripe for the plucking. It was the most sought after book ever written. It was a ledger of legend, a manuscript of myth! Prometheus giggled at his own intellect. Here was what the cat had described as the last and greatest mystery a fading explorer like him could ever hope to unearth. Prometheus picked the book up slowly, letting himself enjoy the euphoric nature of such a rare discovery. He ran his fingers gently over the beautiful spine, the intrinsic folds of the leather that bound it. He breathed in deeply, letting the scent of the pages waft through his senses. He closed his eyes, knowing it would be just for an instant. He did not want to forget this moment, though he knew he could not even if he tried. When he opened his eyes, he gasped. The book in his arms had begun to glow. Had it always been glowing? He did not know why he did not see it at first, but he knew then that it had. The very pages themselves oozed light from some inner pulse. He held the book tightly to his chest, the light flickering in intensity the longer he held it there. Indeed, he would never forget such a moment.

"I have the book!" Prometheus shouted, bouncing off the rocks with the book under tow. He darted from treasure pile to treasure pile, his heartbeat picking up again. "Where are you, cat? I have the book!" he shouted again. He stopped and listened for some quick-witted retort or a snide remark, but nothing. "Damned feline," he grumbled, resolving himself with what he was about to do. He checked the cavern, finding the entrance with ease. He always prided himself with how well he could remember a layout. He nodded to himself, thanked the cat mentally for guiding him here, and promptly turned on his heel and made his way for the exit. The pressing thought of that dragon returning led him to not even feel the slightest bit of shame.

In the farthest reaches of the cave, the cat stood still and immoveable. Of course he had heard the shouts of Prometheus. Of course the man had the book and most likely ran out with it. Yes, the cat knew that it was the book that had brought them here. He blinked, his tail swaying back and forth. Even before they had entered the cavern, the book had been the furthest thing from the cat's mind.

The cat had felt it instantly, like a tugging deep within his being. It was a presence more curious than life itself, a feeling deeper and darker than the cat had ever witnessed. He had not watched as Prometheus bounced his way like an idiot toward the center of the cave. Instead, he set out in search for the source of such a presence. The curiosity was almost eating at him from the inside, burning with a yearning to know. How cruel that there would be something in this cave more juicy than the book itself. Over his many lives and many deaths, the cat figured that he had experienced all there was to life. He figured that the book was his own last great mystery, but mysteries always had a way of unraveling. This feeling, this presence weighing on the cat's chest, was unlike anything he had ever felt.

In the back of the cavern, tucked behind the piles of endless trinkets that filled the dragon's lair, the cat had only found a small opening. His tongue flickered, letting the unknown presence wash over his senses. He did not need more confirmation. Through this tiny little opening before him, hidden away for what tasted like an age, was something the cat was not meant to know about. Who would do such a thing? What creature would be so dastardly as to try and keep such a thing to itself? It was unthinkable and quite off-putting. The cat's chest began to burn a molten hot fury of wanting. He had been alive for so long, it was not right for him to be so curious. It did not matter, though. The cat knew this small hole led somewhere incredible and thus the cat would not rest until he found out exactly where that was.

Still, Prometheus was not wrong to turn and run. The cat sneered in anger, unwilling to admit that the man could do anything right, but in the end his own emotions were futile. In the end there would still be the pressing matter of an upset dragon returning to his lair. The cat sighed and turned to leave, but could not help but hesitate. He cursed himself under his breath, feeling his muscles tense. He felt he could probably take the dragon in the long run, but it was not worth the risk. Not yet, anyway. The cat closed his eyes and hissed soothingly before finally turning tail.

Outside, Prometheus did not even attempt to shield his eyes from the harsh sunlight. He ran from the cave as fast as he could, making straight for the woods. His speed surprised even him. He hit the tree line and dove for the safety of the rocks and thick trunks, thanking whatever god, deity or being that was apparently looking out for him. Just then, a roar tore across the sky. The very clouds above seemed to shiver at the weight of it. Instinctively, Prometheus jumped at the sound, falling straight to the ground. He landed face first in the dirt behind the largest tree in sight. For as bad as it tasted, he could not have been happier. He spit the dirt from his mouth and turned around. The dragon landed swiftly in front of the cave.

He had to admit, it was a terribly majestic creature. Overall, the dragon was as big as a school bus with bright white scales that flittered in the sunlight. He spread his wings like a monstrous peacock and tore the air in two with a gigantic ball of fire. Prometheus quivered in fear, a motion his mind would not let him hear the end of, but still he did not drop the book. He would never drop the book. The book was his.

"I can smell your treachery, Cat!" the dragon roared, his voice as deep as a mountain's roots. Ash and soot dripped from his nostrils as he whipped the ground with his tail. "Get out here!"

The cat emerged almost playfully from the shadows at the cave's mouth. Paw by paw he stepped lightly until finally sitting himself down in the sunlight. The golden grass swayed back and forth around him, glistening against his midnight purple fur. "Hello, again," he said casually, yawning as if nothing were amiss. His tail swayed smoothly back and forth, ticking along to an internal metronome. It always seemed to do that, ever swaying. Prometheus absolutely detested it.

"It's been an age or two," the cat said, licking his paw. "Is something the matter?"

"Don't play coy with me," the dragon said. He lowered his head to the cat's level, his wings spread out like a bat. "Where's the egg?" Flame began to pour from his mouth, singeing the ground below to a crisp. To Prometheus's surprise, the cat did not so much as flinch. He only licked his paw gingerly, pondering exactly what it was that the dragon meant.

"Egg? Hmm, egg. What a wonderful idea!" The cat nodded to himself in recognition. "Now that you mention it, I haven't had a good egg in a century's time." He smiled innocently. "I should look into finding a quail's nest or some other bird whose unbridled offspring I could swallow."

"Enough of your games!" the dragon roared. The grass and ground shattered under the swift crack of his tail. "Did you think that fake trail of yours would last? Do you not understand what hangs in the balance? The egg is more important than your amusement, cat! One dragon, one egg, the cycle must continue!"

"That sounds quite boring," the cat said as he set his paw lightly on the ground. He arched his back in a forged yawn. For an instant, Prometheus could have sworn that the cat had looked at him, but it was just for an instant. Instead, the cat grinned wickedly. "Besides, I think my fake trail lasted exactly as long as I needed it to."

The way the cat leapt from the ground onto the dragon's head was so swift and nimble, Prometheus was not sure it had even happened. As Prometheus watched the dragon's head erupt into a flurry of deep blue flame, though, he knew that indeed it had. The cat leapt and only the blue flame was left, engulfing the dragon's skull in its entirety. The dragon roared, flailing his neck about in anguish. The fire evaporated all at once, leaving a severely angered dragon in its place. All at once the dragon began to slam his tail and forelegs into the ground in unison, sending up vicious columns of earth and ground to wherever the cat attempted to land. The cat was more than aptly nimble, dodging left and right in perfect succession.

While he watched the onslaught of powers that should by no means exist, Prometheus knew he would get no better opportunity to turn tail and run, so to speak. So, he did. Without a second of hesitation, he left the silly magical animals to fight to the death. He smiled to himself. Honestly, he hoped they would.

Later that night, Prometheus found himself shivering and alone in woods he did not know. How long had it been that he had tried to sleep? A gust of wind caught his spine and again he trembled. He knew he dared not chance a fire. In fact, he knew he dared not chance anything except breathing, but some things he could not help but do. He sat up and took the book out of his bag, unable to resist. How many times had he done this now? He did not care. He could not get enough of his new prize, and so he set it on the ground in front of him. At first glance, it was nothing more than a book. It was old, that much was easy to tell, but it certainly did not look special. He reached out and caressed the cover, unable to resist. The book looked as if it had seen more years than the earth itself, yet still it managed to stay together. It was a most unsettling thought, though mainly because it was one he did not understand. Slowly, he began to open the cover.

"I am glad to see that my companion is so overwhelmed with grief that he just could not wait to take off."

Prometheus jumped, shocked at the sight of the cat stepping out from behind a tree. He cursed lightly and gathered himself from his shock. He always hated the way the cat's paws seemed so perfectly silent. He spat, deciding it was now his most hated attribute.

"I shouted to you that I was leaving!" Prometheus said in earnest, gathering himself. "You disappeared, anyways. Where did you go? What more important thing could you have possibly found?"

The cat sniffed. "I haven't the slightest idea what you're talking about."

"Of course you don't," Prometheus laughed. He sat forward, his entire demeanor changing in an instant. "What happened with the beast? How did you get away?"

The cat stared at the book. "The dragon and I came to the conclusion that it was all just a grave misunderstanding and he allowed to me to leave forthwith."

"Always quick with the quips," Prometheus said with a sigh. "What about the egg?"

The cat shrugged. "I never actually took the egg. I just made the beast think that it was gone. Funny how the things we want are always right under our nose, eh?" The cat smiled gently, moving towards the opened book.

"What are you doing?" Prometheus said hurriedly, almost too hurriedly.

The cat scoffed. "Why, I'm relishing in our prize!" he said, his eyes locked onto the old manuscript. He had to admit, it was quite the sight. For centuries the cat had heard of the thing, but he did not think he would actually be taken aback when he finally saw it.

"I am quite pleased," the cat said, nodding to himself in thought. "Now, Prometheus, we must discuss exactly who is going to keep it. I had an idea that—"

In truth, the cat never saw the bullet coming. Judging by the way that the cat dropped to the ground so fluidly after the bullet penetrated his skull, Prometheus knew he had felt the intended effects. He blew away the smoke from the barrel of his silver clad .45 revolver like some brazen cowboy he had always aspired to be before shoving it back into its holster underneath his overcoat. The shot rang through the night, but he did not care. He only chuckled to himself wickedly, pleased with his own cunning.

"Again, thank you for everything," Prometheus said, stepping over the cat's body to pick up the book. He tucked the book back into his satchel, swinging it over his arm. "I'm just sorry that our time together was cut short. You did splendidly, my feline friend." Without a glance back, Prometheus pulled out a compass and set off.

The only thing left moving was the blood spilling forth from the hole in the cat's skull.

CHAPTER ONE

The light broke diligently through the window shades, making the dust infested classroom seem stuffier than it already was. Of the twenty or so eye rubbing, foot shaking, oddball juniors that were doomed to be in Mr. Adrian Everhart's sixth period Modern History class, Derek Richard Agons was the only one not capable of so easily masking his perpetual boredom. His pencil tapped lightly on his desk as his eyes lost focus in the dust dancing playfully against the sunlight. It was not his fault the dust was far more intellectually compelling than the topic at hand, though if he had seen how his eyes were more glazed than a baker's dozen, he probably would have at least blinked.

"Derek?" The voice rang in his head, pulling him from his own blank thoughts. "Would you care to join us?"

Derek diverted his gaze from the sunlight only to find himself being stared down by twenty or so students delighted to find the first non-school-related subject to come along in the last thirty-three minutes. Mr. Everhart stared knowingly, a single eyebrow cocked at Derek's defiance. Derek met his gaze for a moment, but ultimately sunk back into his seat. Mr. Everhart nodded, turning back to his once pristine dry erase board. He was a middling man, though Derek had never found much fault in him. As a teacher, he was never too forceful, though also never too nice, but in the end he was usually fair in his attempts for the betterment of high school education. Derek could have certainly done without the same blue striped, button up shirt and white washed jeans that Mr. Everhart seemed to possess, though Derek knew it did not really matter. It was Modern History, not fashion, which Mr. Everhart was attempting to teach.

"Yes, well, as I was saying," Mr. Everhart said, pointing to a poster pinned on the wall. "Randall Prometheus is the first of four modern day explorers we will begin discussing on Monday."

Derek stared at the poster as he had done for the past few semesters. In it stood a ravishingly tall gentleman with deep blue, piercing eyes and a smile that outshone the sun. Twenty or so scrolls surrounded the man in a flowery fashion, each twisting like a vine around him. His foot was propped on a globe of the world, right in front of the big red letters and deep black drop shadow that promptly pronounced *PROFESSOR RANDALL PROMETHEUS*.

"Furthermore," continued Mr. Everhart, leaning on his desk, "there will be a book signing for Professor Prometheus tonight at Barry's Book Barn, off of Blackman and Thirty-Second Street." Mr. Everhart met Derek's eyes coolly, making sure that Derek was now paying attention. "I will be giving extra credit to all who attend, which may be the difference between whether or not you pass this class." Mr. Everhart let the words hang in the air.

The school bell rang and Derek could feel Mr. Everhart's eyes on him. Quickly, he gathered his things and attempted to sneak out of the class with the other students, already filing out of the door without a moment's hesitation. "Derek?" Mr. Everhart called over the bustling students, "can I see you a moment?" Derek sighed, stopping in his tracks. Reluctantly, he turned on his heel and walked over to Mr. Everhart's desk.

"Yes, Mr. Everhart?" Derek asked, both hands glued to his backpack straps. He met Mr. Everhart's gaze without a second thought, but he already knew what his teacher was going to say.

"I hope to see you at that book signing tonight."

Derek said nothing, his face a stone wall.

"I don't think it's a secret Derek, you could use the extra credit," said Mr. Everhart slowly. He sighed heavily, clearly exasperated with repeating himself. "Look, I'd just hate to see my best student fail."

"I'll think about it," Derek replied, but it was easy to tell by his suddenly slouched posture that the words had hit home. "Can I go now?"

"Of course," said Mr. Everhart, his words trailing in thought. Derek turned to leave.

"Unless there's something you'd like to talk about," Mr. Everhart interjected coolly. Derek stopped. "Family issues? Bullies? Girl problems?"

Derek smiled. "No, I think I'm good."

"Okay then," Mr. Everhart sighed again. He nodded towards the door. "You're free to leave. Hopefully I'll see you tonight."

Derek left the school, taking his normal walking route home. His head bobbed along to the music in his headphones as he let each step on his path take him through back yards, parking lots and alleyways. His mom was not delighted in his particular choice of music, ranging from rap mix tapes to video game remixes, but it was easier for her to turn a blind eye as long as it did not affect his school or attitude. Then again, his mother was so focused on dealing with his siblings and father that in the end, the less she knew the better. Most nights Derek could be found inside his headphones with a video game or a good book in his hands, head always rocking to the beat. It was not that he liked being a loner, for he did not revel in his solitude for any stretch of the imagination, he just really enjoyed the taste of a new world to explore. It helped that it was easier to sustain a train of thought without the presence of needless chattering.

On his pathway home, one particular alleyway was Derek's favorite, if one were to play favorites with paved cement in the first place. It was an unassuming in-between street and an integral part of his true secret path; always quiet and always vacant, even though it connected the two biggest intersections in a seven-mile radius. When he first discovered it, he had claimed it his eye of the hurricane for it was always oddly peaceful though the streets around it raged incessantly.

Today, the eye of the hurricane was not empty.

Derek stopped walking when he noticed a single cat with fur as cold and haunting as the hovering night sitting directly in the middle of his alley, looking outwards towards the street as if surveying it. This was not right. No person, place, nor thing had ever been in Derek's alleyway as long as he could remember. Still, there sat the cat. The oddest thing of all though lay between the cat's paws; a spiraled notebook, the kind schoolgirls use to draw their frilly heart notes of undying love upon.

Slowly, the cat's head turned around as if it already knew Derek was watching him. His tail swayed back and forth methodically, clicking to an internal metronome. Derek could not tell if he was frozen by the cat's slanted golden stare or the fact that he seemed to be taking notes, something even he had not done in forever. Derek blinked as the cat's expression changed. If he had not known better, he would have sworn he saw the cat raise an eyebrow at him.

The cat stretched out on all fours, swirled his head back around and gathered up the spiraled notebook in its mouth. The cat's paws made no sound as he casually padded away, leaving Derek with a queasy stomach and a mountain of unanswerable questions.

When Derek arrived home, he threw his backpack by the door and plopped down on the living room couch, his normal resting place. He did not remember grabbing the remote, but the television in front of him turned on nonetheless and the remote control was in his hand. The entire action was completely muscle memory at this point.

". . . And in other news, America is yet again recoiling in turmoil from yet another seemingly natural disaster." Derek opened the bag of chips in his lap, not remembering when he had picked them up in the first place. He let the sound of the television news anchor wash over him. "An earthquake in the southern Phoenix, Arizona area. The quake today, measuring in at a 6.2, sets a new record for the highest amount of tremors in a three month period. This, coupled with the increasing hurricanes along the East Coast, begs for an answer as to the source of these natural disasters." The television flashed horrific videos of the incidents, grabbing Derek's interest. Entire coastal cities were being bombarded with raging storms, wild fires were spreading at an alarming rate across the coldest of climates as they ripped through tree and snow alike while earthquakes split apart the earth underneath like it was paper. He sipped from the soda can in his hand, his eyebrows raised slightly in attention. If there were an end of the world scenario, it would probably look something very similar to this. ". . . Some of the more outspoken religious groups are claiming Armageddon, rapture and possibly biblical retribution on the earth," the reporter continued on in his monotone drawl, "but we now take it to Matthew Perrile, our senior scientific correspondent, who claims to know the exact scientific correlation between the earth's core and the natural disasters themselves. Mr. Perrile —"

The television set clicked off.

"Hey!" Derek said with a start. He turned to face the culprit. "I was watching that."

Derek's mother stood in the kitchen doorway, wielding the all-powerful remote control in her hand. With her apron tied around her chest like a breastplate, her hair in her usual ponytail and smears of some dish she was failing to make for dinner pasted on her cheeks, Mary Catherine Agons seemed to carry herself like an old warrior chief, always ready for the inevitable battle. She sniffed slightly, surveying Derek as she brushed a loose strand of her fading chocolate brown hair behind her ear. She was not pleased with what she saw.

"I need you to watch Robbie tonight," Mary's voice rang out in that sweet but commanding tone that every mother's child knows too well.

Derek could not help but flinch. "I can't watch him tonight."

"Of course not," she said, doing her best to withhold an eye roll. She failed.

"I don't need anyone to watch me!" Derek's little brother said as he stormed into the living room battlefield. His arms were firmly planted across his chest in defiance as if daring someone to babysit him. Derek smiled slightly at the sight. Robbie had just hit his first awkward stage, the one filled with defiance in everything, right before the peach fuzz, acne and sweat in odd places.

"We've been over this, Robbie," replied Mary, her patience waning. "You need a sitter until I say you don't."

Robbie's brow furrowed as he huffed indignantly. "Then I'm not moving ever again," he said, shaking his head and sitting directly onto the floor. Derek was not surprised to see that through all of this, Robbie's arms were still inexplicably crossed.

"Again with the sitting thing," Mary said in exasperation. She turned to Derek. "You're babysitting him and that's final."

"Mom, I really can't!" Derek said as she turned back into the kitchen. "I have to go to an extra credit thing for school or . . ."

Mary stopped, turning slowly on her heel. Bit by bit, she began to rub her neck as if a momentary self-massage could ease any of the building tension. "Or what, Derek?" Her piercing blue eyes shot straight threw him. Regardless of any fading beauty, Derek knew his mother would always retain that incredible glare.

"Or else I might fail." He looked his mother in the eye as every word poured out. Honestly, he was rather proud of himself for finally telling the truth, though it was a small victory with what was about to come.

His mother's face remained completely expressionless as she processed the words. She nodded slightly. Derek could feel his mother's gaze as she weighed the consequences.

"Fine, we will deal with you later," she said with a sniff. "Elizabeth, I need you to watch Robbie tonight."

Derek's older sister, Elizabeth, sat on the couch next to Derek, trying her best not to be noticed. Once upon a time, Elizabeth was an ever-growing symbol of the youthful beauty that their mother once possessed, but that went away quickly with Elizabeth's freshman year of college as she discovered how pizza, snack food and a healthy supply of cheap beer lead to the freshmen fifteen.

Elizabeth glared at her mother, mouth agape in shock. "I'm not watching him. I have plans too."

"I don't need to be watched!" Robbie shouted again. Derek was surprised to see his little brother still sitting directly on the floor; usually his protests barely lasted thirty seconds.

"Yes, you do!" Mary shouted back before calming herself with three deep breaths. "Someone has to watch him," she soldiered on. "I finally have your father for a night and I'm taking him out!" She looked to her children desperately, her eyes pleading. "Please? Someone?"

Robbie and Derek's heads swiveled towards Elizabeth in unison.

"Fine," said Elizabeth, drawing out the single syllable word into four long ones. She sat back, crossing her arms in resignation. "I'll do it."

"Thank you," Mary said, clicking the television back on as she returned to the kitchen.

And so, the three Agons children sat and watched television until it was time for Derek to finally leave. He offered his mother another apology, greeted by only a dejected shrug, before grabbing his backpack, wallet and car keys and heading out the front door. As he left, he noticed Robbie sitting in the exact same place, arms still crossed, only moving his head enough to see the television. Derek was really rather impressed.

When Derek pulled up to Barry's Book Barn later that night, he was surprised to find it completely packed. The bookstore itself was unassuming in stature, a medium sized brick and mortar store that oozed of self-published works at first glance, but even the nicer buildings surrounding it seemed feeble against the massive line of people stacked up the street. Each person seemed to sway in time with the other's impatient shuffling as they murmured excitedly to one another. Derek pulled into the parking lot, finding it completely full. He offered himself a light whistle in comment, before pulling out and driving what must have been half a mile down the street until a space finally opened up.

He pushed his way through to the front door, noting the intricately strange inhabitants of the crowd. Each man was either deplorably tall or inexplicably short, fashioning themselves with tangled meshes of hair that fell lightly off the chin or curly mustaches that tickled the higher parts of the cheekbone. Their eyes were covered with oddly shaped reading glasses that rested on the edge of noses both pointy and stout. One man even wore rosewood, star shaped spectacles. They chewed on twisting pipes and busty cigars that smelled of the most singeing combinations of exotic tobacco, talking through each puff in seemingly self-dignified prose. The women, who were not to be outshone on any level of outlandish customs, were clothed in the brightest of fabrics, each drab and baggy dress a new splash of vibrant color that hung loosely to the floor. They too fancied themselves with cigars and pipes, their shrill voices congressing into a high pitched mesh as it entered Derek's ear. He was surprised that the women did not have beards themselves.

Finally, Derek pushed his way inside. For its drab and seemingly dull appearance on the outside, Barry's Book Barn's insides were quite lavish in contrast. The entirety of the store was laced with a bright white marble that clung effortlessly along each wall as they raced to meet in the open and gigantic crescent ceiling overhead. Twisting staircases bounded their way across three stories worth of bookshelves, piled onwards and upwards, filled with manuscripts and texts as seemingly ancient as the wooden bookcases that held them. A quaint little table sat perfectly placed in the middle of the store, purposefully for Professor Prometheus's signing. He looked around and shook his head. There was no way the majority of the crowd piled outside would actually fit in such a small space. He smiled slightly, nodding in approval, and walked through the nearest set of doors to seek out the nearest bathroom.

As he washed his hands and walked out, a group of frustrated murmurs caught Derek's ear. The mutterings rang loudly through the desolate and twisting hallways before him, though the subject matter itself was indistinguishable. Derek could not help but find himself curious. Cautiously, he followed the voices, poking his head around the corner to investigate.

To his surprise, he found his teacher Mr. Everhart deep in the midst of a whispering match against a man of rather striking stature. Instantly, Derek recognized the man in question as Professor Randall Prometheus himself with his jet white hair and eyes that could search out the soul of any subject unlucky enough to fall under their gaze. The conversation seemed like a one-way battle, with the professor doing most of the heated whispering.

The professor noticed Derek and immediately stopped talking, staring in Derek's direction. Mr. Everhart followed the man's gaze hurriedly, but his steel resolution melted away as he realized who was spying in on the conversation.

"Derek!" Mr. Everhart exclaimed. "I'm so glad you could make it." Mr. Everhart signaled Derek over, smiling warmly. Derek obliged, though hesitantly. He could not help but wish to distance himself from Prometheus's most disconcerting stare. Derek felt as if the professor had already read Derek's character to the tee, striking down his every wish, will and weak point.

"I'd like you to meet an old friend of mine," Mr. Everhart continued happily, greeting Derek warmly with open arms. He turned toward the white haired man at his shoulder, his face all smiles. "Derek," he beamed, "this is Professor Randall Prometheus."

Derek extended his hand slowly, his heart beginning to race, but Prometheus's face broke into an even bigger smile than Mr. Everhart's as he shook Derek's hand, even going so far as to pat the top of Derek's hand with his unoccupied one. Derek's fears melted in the face of such warmness. Prometheus's gaze was piercing, to be sure, but his smile was undeniably welcoming. Derek scolded himself for being so silly.

"Nice to finally meet you, Derek," Prometheus said sincerely, his smile ever-growing. "Adrian has told me a lot about you."

"Adrian?" Derek asked, bewildered and a little taken aback. He could have sworn he had just seen Prometheus's eyes actually twinkle.

"I do have a first name, you know," Mr. Everhart said as he and Prometheus shared a laugh.

"Oh, right," Derek said slowly. "Sorry, Mr. Everhart." He could not seem to move his eyes away from Prometheus no matter how hard he tried.

"Oh, Mr. Everhart, eh?" Prometheus said, nudging his good friend. "I do not think I'll ever get used to that."

Derek smiled awkwardly as the two apparently old friends shared another laugh together. Prometheus checked his watch, nodding to himself as he basked in their joviality. "Well then, I do believe it is time for me to sign some autographs," he said, his face beaming. "I do hope you two would join me?"

"We'd be delighted, Randall," Mr. Everhart beamed back.

Prometheus stared down at Derek, the wrinkles under his eyes whispering about the many great and terrible adventures the warm and gentle explorer could tell, but it was the violent blue pupils that occupied the space above them that still made Derek uneasy. Prometheus's eyes seemed to smirk relentlessly with no regards to what position his lips were in. "Derek?"

"Yeah, of course." Derek followed them closely as they marched together down the empty hallways, laughing and reminiscing.

When the double doors gave way to Professor Prometheus, the deafening noise of the impatient crowd bursting into applause swept over Derek like a flood.

High above the spiraling staircases and dilapidated shelves filled with human nonsense in paperback form, six small bars of light escaped through a particular air vent's slanted gate. Two golden eyes glistened in the glow's brilliance, though in truth they always seemed to shine like cascading fountains.

A singular cat with fur as black as night sat hunched within the air vent, yawning as he tried to stretch out his aching back. Casually, he surveyed the strange throng of humans that filled Barry's Book Barn below. How silly it

was, the cat thought to himself, that they would wait all this time for a single man whose compiled expeditions did not even make for that great of a read. Yet, still he waited patiently for this man to show himself.

A sudden eruption of applause from the crowd below piqued that cat's interest. The doors across the lobby had opened as the man named Prometheus waltzed in gloriously, followed by another man not so important. This much the cat had expected. What the cat had not expected was the boy who followed behind them. The cat knew he had seen that boy before, but figuring out when exactly became a fleeting thought as Prometheus took his seat at the signing table.

He slung his satchel off his shoulder in a flourish, setting it beside his chair as the first lucky enthusiast approached. He smiled and reached down to open his bag, pulling out his favorite quill pen. Just for a second, a slight golden light emanated from within the bag, a pulsating luminance that whispered of secrets. Prometheus closed his bag quickly, making sure no one had seen as he turned back to his awaiting fans.

But the cat saw. The cat saw everything.

As the last braided beard walked out the door with his precious autograph in hand, Prometheus stood from his chair and surveyed the cleared out bookstore in front of him. He smoothed his vibrant yellow khakis, stretching longingly. "That went well," he yawned, turning to Mr. Everhart. "Wouldn't you say so, Adrian?"

"It went quite well indeed," Mr. Everhart said, patting his old friend on the back. Mr. Everhart smiled proudly.

"What did you think, Derek? Did you enjoy yourself?" Prometheus asked, without giving so much as a glance to Derek's person, though Derek did not particularly mind.

"Yes sir," Derek replied quickly with a nod.

"Oh! Adrian, I almost forgot," Prometheus said, picking up his satchel with a jolt, "I have something for

you." Randall thrust a hand into the tattered bag he always carried, his eyes twinkling in delight. "I picked this up on one of my many adventures."

The blood drained from Prometheus's face. In a flash, he ripped through the bag, searching furiously. Horrified, he dropped to his knees and turned the bag over, spilling its innards across the floor, rustling his fingers frantically through the mess of odd trinkets, pieces of parchment and worldly currencies. His eyes bulged from their sockets as a thick vein began to pulse noticeably on his forehead.

"Where is it? Where is it?!" he screamed, scouring through the empty bookstore with his eyes. He tore again and again through the pile of trinkets on the floor, but to no avail. "Where the hell is it!?" He pounded his fists on the ground in a futile rage.

Mr. Everhart looked around nervously as a store clerk began to race over. "Randall, please do calm down," he said, wringing his hands anxiously. "I'm sure that whatever you had for me isn't that important—"

"—Not your stupid trinket, Adrian!" Prometheus raged, turning his anger on his old friend. He stood, throwing his now empty satchel at Mr. Everhart. "The book, you idiot! It's gone!"

Mr. Everhart looked around, trying helplessly to assess the situation. "Ah, Derek!" he said, enveloping Derek in an open arm and a shaky smile. "I think it's about time you went home," he laughed nervously as he turned Derek away from the scene and towards the door. "No need to be out so late and worry your parents!"

"Yeah, uh, about the whole extra credit thing," Derek hesitated, his eyes glued over his shoulder on Prometheus as the crazed man turned on unwitting two store clerks, "do I need something signed or will you just count that I was here?"

"Your extra credit has been taken care of," Mr. Everhart insisted irritably. He shoved Derek to the door. "Now go home, please."

"I just want to make sure I pass and everything like you said—"

"—You will be fine, Derek!" Mr. Everhart shouted. "Okay? I will see you in class."

With one last stolen glance at the supposedly great Professor Prometheus, who was now violently shaking one of the poor workers of Barry's Book Barn by the collar, screaming loud threats of how he would burn in a lake of sulfuric hellfire if they did not find the Professor's supposed book, Mr. Adrian Everhart closed the door on an increasingly curious Derek Agons.

Derek made his way across the lonesome parking lot, now empty and vacant. The night itself was a splash of welcomed cold against Derek's face. He steadied his breathing and let his mind race. The great Prometheus was quite an excitable fellow, to be sure. He kicked at a rock and crossed under the soft yellow pools of the parking lot lights, commenting under his breath at how they swirled against the booming moonlight from the night sky. Suddenly, a gust of wind sent a shiver down his spine. He covered himself in his jacket. Just because his face enjoyed the cold did not mean the rest of him reveled in it.

As he walked across the parking lot, the sounds of Prometheus's screaming that rang through Barry's Book Barn walls and into his ears quickly gave way to another new sound: a murmuring, as if someone was hurriedly talking to himself as his temper raised. The murmuring became almost audible and Derek could have sworn he heard someone curse. He turned around, seeking out this new voice, only to find a cat as black as the night walking hurriedly across the parking lot. In his mouth, he pulled along what seemed to Derek to be a very old and dilapidated book. The cat clawed and pushed with every ounce of his strength as he tried to drag the book along. Derek blinked in astonishment. Either his eyes were playing tricks on him, or the cat's fur had begun to glisten from the glow escaping from deep within the book's pages.

A gust of wind betrayed Derek. The cat caught his scent, whipping around to face him. Instantly, his back arched in instinct. His head was down and focused as he stood over the book. The cat's tail began to sway back and forth as if to some internal metronome. His bright golden eyes locked onto Derek in an instant, twinkling lavishly as they caught the book's inner glow.

Derek hesitated, knowing he had seen those eyes before. This was the same cat from earlier, the same cat that had crowded his usually deserted pathway home. Derek stood up, knowing his face must have been a silly sight of complete puzzlement, though it was nothing compared to the cat's face of equal questioning. If Derek had not known better, he could have sworn that the cat seemed to recognize him, too. Ever so slightly, the cat's head tilted sideways as his posture relaxed and his tail stopped swaying, if only for a second.

A gut-wrenching screech ripped through the air, piercing Derek's skull to the core. He dropped to the ground, covering his ears with his hands, trying to shake the vibrations off. He looked up as two blazing white streaks of feathers dropped from the sky like miniature meteorites, talons first. The cat twisted to face the new threat, but Derek could tell it was too late. Nothing could stop the owls on their descent. The cat disappeared into the night sky, his body speared across two different sets of owl claws, leaving only the sound of the claws ripping through flesh and muscle ringing in Derek's head.

He forced himself to breathe as he stood up straight and scanned the night air for the possibility of another attack. He counted in his head, wondering how long would need to pass before he felt safe. His knees began to wobble underneath him. After a minute-long eternity passed, an eerie silence settled in over the parking lot. He looked around nervously though he knew now that he was yet again alone.

His eyes met the book now lying peacefully where the cat had once stood. Even from a distance the odd book seemed to pulsate from within. Slowly, he made his way to it, examining the sky with every step. As he drew closer, his brow furrowed at the sight of it. The book itself was absolutely magnificent. From afar, the book had seemed like another unassuming assortment of dusty pages he would never read, but the closer he drew to it the more the book aged. He wondered how the cover could possibly still be bound; the book seemed as if it had seen every age of mankind.

Strangest of all, though, was how the pages were actually glowing. He assumed it must have been another trick of the light, but now that he was so close, he could almost feel the book's warmth on his skin. He crouched down to get a closer look, letting his knees rest on the pavement. The book was akin to that of a firefly, the pages breathing light from some unknown internal source.

Hesitantly, Derek gathered the book in his arms. At first, he was afraid that the dilapidated manuscript might crumble into dust between his fingers, but the longer he held onto it, he knew the book's strength. He glanced at the sky again. Still nothing. Cautiously, he opened the cover.

Instantly, the glow faded away. Derek looked on in shock. Blank. Completely blank. He quickly thumbed through the rest of the book's rough and jagged pages, but still nothing. Every page was entirely void of any sort of picture, text or manuscript.

The sound of bones crunching against the pavement lurched Derek back to reality as a black object thundered down from the sky, landing directly in front of him with a crunch. He forced himself to look, though somehow he already knew what had fallen beside him. An arm's length away laid the lifeless body of the cat, spread out limp across the pavement. The poor animal's bones were mangled from the impact, his legs twisting underneath him in ways that sent Derek's stomach reeling. Blood poured forth from the two gaping talon wounds. Again, Derek forced himself to breathe. He stood at the ready, his eyes glued to the lifeless animal in front of him. Slowly he walked over to the cat, the book wrapped tightly in his arms.

The cat's eyes were glazed over by the sweet grip of an easy death.

With one last paranoid glance at the sky, Derek left the cat in a pool of blood, his newfound secret tucked neatly beneath his arm.

CHAPTER TWO

The two owls barreled through the sky victoriously, hooting as they twirled through an endless sea of clouds. Their wings flapped in earnest, each rushing to be the first to catch each new gale of wind. The night sky cracked beneath the sound of their proud hooting. They spread their wings and let the wind do the work, culling the air currents around them into unified jet streams. To the naked eye, the two owls were almost impossible to catch as they carried on through the night sky for what seemed like an eternity. The owls did not care. They were proud of their work, proud of finally finding the traitor. Eventually, they finally came upon their destination, a forest as dense, wide and ancient as the mountains surrounding it.

In the middle of the forest sat a particularly large clump of trees, its canopy tied together in a neat little section of knots directly at the branches, so as to form a sort of dome. To those not in on the secret, this dome seemed like another unassuming clump of foliage from vine to vine, offering no real threat or oddities. However, to those animals that still remembered, it was the last gathering place for the most ancient of secrets.

The owls closed their wings, dropping like stones through the foliage into a group of deceivingly thick leaves that parted the second the owls drew near. They landed high above the forest floor on a soft clump of grass, fashioned in the form of a landing patch. The leaves above them began to rustle as a sort of squeaking sound escaped from within. Three squirrels, each with identical buckteeth and rich maroon fur, poked their heads out of the leaves. They squinted in unison, their large eyes darting back and forth as they surveyed the owls below them.

"Names? Names?" the squirrels said in quick succession, twitching back and forth from owl to owl. Together, their heads twisted sideways with each word, so as to get a good read on the trespassers.

The first owl stepped forward. "Bartholomew reporting. Owl-Watch number fourteen."

The second owl joined Bartholomew. "Eustace reporting. Owl-Watch number three."

The trio of squirrels disappeared for a moment before dropping from the overhead leaves onto the branch in front of them. Their large bushy tails twitched back and forth as they turned around to the massive tree behind them. The three squirrels crawled forward together in a perfect triangle, each patting their paws nervously.

"Business? Business?" they said, heads still bobbing. The first squirrel bounced forward, landing on its back legs in a stretch. The other squirrels looked at each other, chirping in query.

Bartholomew stepped forward. "We must see the council immediately," he said, puffing his feathers.

"Th-they are in a meeting!" the first squirrel said.

"Meeting! Meeting!" the other squirrels chirped.

"No one disturbs meetings." The first squirrel shook its head emphatically.

"No one, no one!" the other squirrels chirped.

"But we must report!" Eustace said, stepping forward. "The cat is dead." The owl's gray beak glinted, catching the moonlight in the ensuing silence.

The squirrels looked at each other nervously. Slowly, the first squirrel nodded its head as the other two joined in. "So be it," the squirrel said and, in a flash, the three squirrels disappeared into the treetops.

The great tree in front of the owls began to groan as it shook softly, its bark parting ways directly in the middle to reveal a hollow tree trunk and a hidden passage.

Deep inside, at the very center of the twisted tree trunk tunnels, small shafts of light broke through the overhead thicket of treetops, cascading gently upon the great council's meeting place. It was the largest shroud of trees in the surrounding forest and the thickest there was to offer. Many council cycles ago, those with the first knowledge had chosen the spot for the secrecy it provided, carving out a perfect room from branches, tree trunks and foliage. It gave easy cover from wandering eyes, needless questions, and, more importantly, the flying metal monstrosities that men were known to use. Abraham hated planes. He remembered the day that first wretched metal dragon took flight. He also remembered the day that one took his firstborn son to the grave with it. Abraham clicked a talon on the root in front of him in annoyance.

"Well, Abraham?" Alladin the rat said sharply. "Are you going to answer me or not?"

Abraham sighed. It was unsettling how easy his mind wandered, especially in these troubled times. Sure, Alladin had the right to be annoyed, with almost all of his fellow rats at the point of forgetting, but Abraham would still rather find him on a dinner plate instead of the great council.

"There is nothing more the council can offer you, Alladin," Abraham said, exasperated. He ruffled his feathers in earnest. "I have oft repeated that we are all in troubled times. There are very few of us who remember the old ways, as it is up to the individual, not the collective, who decides to forget and who does not."

From another spot in the dark treetop room, a panther leaned forward, the light bouncing off of her dark purple coat as if the fur itself wanted no part of it. She snarled at Alladin in disdain. "We can't help it if your brethren would rather crawl on their bellies in the trash than remain among the civilized."

The rat bared his fangs, his tail smashing on the ground in anger. "Retract that statement stale-tail or you'll regret it!" Alladin screamed, his voice quivering.

Pathos, panther that she was, bared her fangs in fulfillment. "Just try it. I dare you."

"Enough!" Abraham boomed in his most commanding tone, one that only a great gray owl could muster. He spread his ancient fourteen-foot wingspan, his feathers captivating all who dared to look. "We do not convene to squabble amongst ourselves like men," his voice shook through the treetops. "We convene to make the best out of a terrible situation."

"As you say," the panther said. She rested her head on her paws and retracted from the shafts of light. Alladin quickly sat himself amongst his kin, eyes still glued to Pathos. The rat's mouth foamed in a wordless anger, but he too knew better than to speak out again.

"Now," the great gray owl named Abraham said, folding his wings decidedly underneath him. "We move on to why the great council was called. As of late, there has been an unprecedented spike in natural disasters. Man thinks this is just anomaly, but we know different. Xiu-Fao?"

A monstrous panda bear leaned forward, his eyes sunk into a dim red glare, slanted at the sides. In the darkened canopy room, one could not gauge an accurate size for the panda bear, but judging from how his entire head was bigger than three of the rats put together, the beast must have been huge. The panda spat out the bamboo in his mouth, licking his nose.

"It's the dragon again," the panda bear said in more of a grumble than a set of words.

The council broke into a flurry of confused chatter. "But he hasn't been heard from in hundreds of years! Hundreds!" Albertus the squirrel minister shouted as he bobbed his head in time to his people.

"Impossible!" screamed Alladin.

Pathos looked excited.

"And how do we know it is the dragon?" Abraham clicked his beak in exasperation, though his voice still soothed the raging storm. The council hushed quickly to listen.

"It's him," said Xiu-Fao, clearing his throat. "Our watchers have reported sightings in sporadic bits, but we know it's him."

Suddenly, the gigantic door shaped cropping of thorns rustled away as three squirrel guards dropped down from the treetops, helping move it with haste. Eustace and Bartholomew waddled through the opening. Abraham sighed as the council broke into another chaotic banter, outraged that anyone would even dare to intrude on their most holy of holies.

"What is the meaning of this?" growled Pathos. She sneered at the owl scouts.

Abraham lifted a wing for silence. "Eustace? Bartholomew? This better be worth the interruption."

"It is, sire," began Eustace as he inched forward.

The council grew silent. The rats shifted their weaselly gaze in time with Alladin. Xiu-Fao sat back, ripping off a piece of bark from the nearest tree.

"Well?" asked Abraham, his patience waning.

The two owls looked to each other before the one named Bartholomew stepped forward. "The fugitive has been taken care of," he said, the second owl nodding his approval.

"You're certain?" asked Abraham. He turned his head upside down, bobbing in curiosity.

"We are certain," said Bartholomew. "We know it was his ninth life."

"The cat is dead," Eustace finished.

The council breathed collectively.

"I am elated," said Abraham. "This is the first piece of good news this council has had in a very long time." Abraham ruffled his feathers, puffing his chest. The council agreed in a delighted murmur.

"Now, back on the subject of the dragon," Abraham nodded, quieting the council again. "Have our delegates found out his demands?"

Xiu-Fao's eyes grew murky as he leaned his head backwards. Abraham did not like the tone of his posture one bit. "The book has been stolen."

As the weight of a millennium began to set on his shoulders, Abraham was not surprised to hear the questioning chatter that arose. For once, the great gray owl wished his fellow animals would have actually broken into a roar at the news. At least then, Abraham would not have been able to feel the deep thud that was the pounding of his own heart.

"Book? What book?" Alladin shouted over the growing noise. "Dragons do not read." The rat smiled wickedly at his own cunning. His fellow rats laughed with him at that, though not even their high pitch squeaking could shake the doom growing in the great gray owl's chest.

Abraham made eye contact with both Xiu-Fao and Pathos, the three of them being the only ones present to understand exactly what it meant. Few alive still knew the purpose of the dragon, and even then only slightly. Their terrifying race had always been one for secrecy.

"Did you say a book?"

The room grew quiet. The two owl scouts looked to each other, their beaks clicking nervously. It was the second scout that had spoken up, but it looked as if he wished he had not. Every eye was now honed directly on him.

"That's right, a book," said Xiu-Fao slowly. The sound of the panda bear's voice sent visible shivers down the two owls' spines.

Bartholomew looked to Eustace for some shred of help. "Well," Eustace began as he tapped his talons together, "we saw a book." Bartholomew nodded enthusiastically.

"We've all seen a book," Alladin said. The council chuckled nervously.

"Right, but, the cat had a book," added Bartholomew. The chuckling stopped.

Abraham forced himself to breathe, to be steadfast and calm like a leader should. "And?" he asked. The word hung in the air.

"Well, uh, it was old," Eustace said, nodding to himself.

"Quite right, very old," Bartholomew agreed, adding his own nodding to the equation.

"Anything else?" Abraham was growing impatient.

"It also seemed to . . . glow."

For the last time that day, the room broke into a flurry of questioning chatter, though the tension between the great gray owl, the panda bear and the panther was worse than death itself. An entire millennium had just punched them squarely in the stomach.

The great gray owl forced himself to breath. He raised a wing and the council grew silent. "Where is the book now?" he asked as serenely as he could muster.

Eustace licked his beak nervously. "We don't know."

Bartholomew nodded. "A boy took it."

Abraham let the sting of that settle, keeping his emotions in check. Every eye in the council was now on him. "Do you remember the exact spot you saw the book last?" he asked with complete composure. He allowed himself a slight nod, proud of the way his voice sounded.

"Of course, sire," said Bartholomew with a bow.

"Good," Abraham nodded. "Quinn?"

A menacing mangle of pelt devoid of any and all color emerged from the darkest corner of the room into a single shaft of light. Its fangs flashed as they caught the shimmering particles. The wolf's head rolled nonchalantly from side to side. A single deep purple eye glistened under the shine, blinking the filth and bile out as it raised an eyebrow in answer.

The great gray owl nodded his approval, readying himself for whatever lay ahead. "Send your best," he said to the wolf. "We have to find that book."

With a slight grin and a wicked growl, the wolf named Quinn nodded in reply.

CHAPTER THREE

That night, in his quiet little home tucked away at the end of his quaint little street, Derek Agons found it absolutely impossible to find sleep. He tossed and turned as his mind raced, reliving each and every intricate detail of the events that had just passed. He kicked and twisted until his bed became nothing but a sweaty mess of sheets. He flipped his pillow on its side, hoping the change of pace would offer some solitude, but to no avail. Regardless of what he tried, he could not shake the book from his mind.

He closed his eyes and there it was. He drifted off and there it was. He rolled over and still there it was, an ancient text pulsing from deep within its leather confines. He opened his eyes and found the book sitting playfully on the edge of his desk where he had left it. For some reason now, the book stood still in the darkness, offering no glow or hint of luminance. He wondered if he had imagined it, but then he remembered the sound of the cat hitting the pavement and knew that even his overactive imagination could not have dreamed this one up. He had gotten into his car, hands shaking as he started it, wondering how he did not get pulled over. In truth, he did not exactly remember the drive itself. The entire trip was nothing more than a hazy memory. All he could remember was that the book had never left the security of his tucked arm. For some reason, he felt like he had to protect the blank pages and whatever secrets they held, and he was absolutely certain those secrets would be worth it. The second he finally pulled into his own driveway, he screeched to a halt, rushing past his mother with a solitary greeting and going straight to his room. Instantly, he locked the door and placed the book on his desk in easy reading territory, though he found himself unwilling to touch it again. For the better part of an hour, he failed to do his homework. For the lesser part of an hour, he just stared at the book. He rolled over again, scolding himself as the thoughts twisted and gnarled in his brain. It was just a book, regardless of how it fell into his hands. How silly he must have looked, staring blankly at the ramshackle manuscript, too scared and too timid to actually open it.

The covers flew off with a determined kick. Derek leapt from his bed and brought himself to face the book again. He sat down at his desk, turning on his desk lamp with an emphatic click. Without thinking, he grabbed for the book but his hand hesitated as it hovered over the cover. He readied himself. Again, he thought himself silly, for it truly was just a book. He forced both hands to grab the hardback and place it directly in front of him. He could feel his heart thumping along in his chest. With a deep breath, he grabbed his lamp and examined the manuscript from end to end, his nose almost touching the odorless leather covering. The book itself was sort of an oddity; it bared no title, no author, no illustrated signs of its birthright. He ran a finger down the spine to the outer edge of the front cover and opened it, already knowing what he would find there.

Nothing. Just like in the parking lot, the book was completely blank. Derek chewed on his lip, staring back at the vacant pages in front of him. Quickly, he leafed through them with a thumb and forefinger, searching for some sort of word or indication of origin. Again, nothing. Derek reached for the back cover of the book and began to thumb through it in reverse, hoping for different results but still finding none. The book was absolutely void of any ink, lead or acrylic from cover to cover. No words, no pictures, no descriptions or dedications, just an endless sea of fading white paper.

Derek clicked the light off and crawled his way back into his bed defeated and somewhat deflated, which helped keep the curiosity at bay long enough for his mind to finally find rest.

The next day at school, Derek found himself having an even worse time concentrating. He bounced from class to class in the hallways, speaking even less to his peers than normal. The classes themselves dragged on and on as he trudged through each period, filling each of his schoolbooks with doodles of recklessly plummeting owls, glowing books and dead cats. His teachers' words slid past his ears as he missed important homework assignments and even began to draw on a pop quiz. He could not help it; it was like the book was a shield to outside thoughts in general. Blank or not, it was stuck to Derek's forethoughts. Nothing of the real world, the world Derek thought he knew, could possibly penetrate.

By the time the bell rang for lunch, the gnawing secrets that the book had to hold could not be repressed. Derek scanned the cafeteria for an empty table and hurried over to it, not even bothering to bring out his lunch. The book consumed his appetite. He opened up his bag and pulled the book from within, resting it on the table in front of him. Quickly, he scanned the cafeteria for prying eyes, but no one seemed to care. He cracked open the cover and leafed to the front page, his eyes closed with hope. He steadied his breathing, wishing and praying for something, anything from the book, but when he opened his eyes still he was greeted with nothing. The book was as blank as it ever was. He sighed, lifting his eyes from the book in thought. He was disappointed to be sure, but what had he really expected? Magic words to form on blank pages? A picture of a faraway land that would whisk him away from his droll life to a place filled with fantastical adventure? Maybe some sort of secret code that let only him in on the beginnings of the universe or a treasure map leading to an unknown prize that only he could ever obtain? He scoffed at himself. That was all silly, childish nonsense.

His mind wondered about the endless possibilities, of pirates and fairies and other ridiculous things, until a girl caught Derek's eye. She shined brightly in the white linen dress she wore, her hair a lump of shoulder length light auburn curls. She was naturally beautiful, oddly surrounded by the painted faces of teenage females who pretended to not know she existed. She smiled, and Derek realized suddenly that she was staring directly back at him. He blushed and diverted his gaze at first, but he shyly met her peaceful look again. Together, they locked eyes and Derek found he was unable to help himself. Still she sat and still she stared directly back at him, her face a peaceful sea in which he could drown. She tilted her head in a curious fashion as her smile grew. Derek smiled back weakly. She raised a finger and pointed directly over Derek's shoulder.

"Hello, Derek." Derek jumped, surprised at the voice he knew all too well. Quickly, he turned, only to find Mr. Everhart standing over him with a warm smile and crossed arms. His eyes were glued on the book.

"Hi, Mr. Everhart," Derek said, gathering his composure. He cleared his throat, his mind already itching to look back to the girl. "What can I do for you?" Coolly, he closed the book behind him, offering the same warm smile Mr. Everhart gave him.

"Oh, nothing, just on cafeteria duty today," Mr. Everhart said in reply. He licked his lips unconsciously, his slight mustache dancing under the nervous movement of his tongue. "That is a very interesting book you have there,

Derek. It's not a school book, is it?" The seemingly innocent question hung in the air.

"Yes, actually it is," Derek replied calmly. "It's an old book I got for Spanish class on settlers and colonies, that sort of thing." He shrugged. "Miss Coller thinks it'll help out with the language, though it's kind of old and boring to me."

"May I see it?" Mr. Everhart stuck out his hand.

"O-of course," Derek hesitated, before handing it over.

Mr. Everhart turned the book over in his hands, his eyes stoic and unblinking. He examined the cover closely, eyebrows furrowed in concentration. He ran a finger down the spine and shivered. "This is a very old book Derek," he began. "Where did you get it?"

"I just told you," Derek said, his face as cool as his tone. "Miss Coller gave it to me for Spanish."

"Interesting, very interesting," Mr. Everhart said as he pursed his lips. Slowly, he peeled back the cover, his hands trembling in anticipation.

"Don't!" Derek blurted out, unable to stop himself.

Mr. Everhart glared at him in response, his eyebrows raised in intrigue.

"I don't want you to lose my place," Derek said. He extended his hand out.

Mr. Everhart's face darkened. "Of course," he said, reluctantly handing the book back. Derek swiftly placed the book in his bag.

"Well, I'll see you in class, then." Mr. Everhart stared at Derek's backpack.

"Yeah, see you in class," Derek repeated. Mr. Everhart turned on his heel and carried himself indignantly out of the cafeteria.

Derek waited for a minute before daring to glance back to where the girl had been, but she was no longer there. Slightly dejected, Derek pulled out his lunch. Almost simultaneously, the exit bell rang. He sighed to himself and then carried on his day with a growling stomach and a head full of questions.

When Derek finally arrived home from school, he pushed past his kitchen bound mother with a quick *"Homework"* and ran down stairs to the garage. The stock answer *"Homework"* was one Derek pulled out often these days, though it was usually reserved for when he wanted alone time and did not care to watch any television. He found that many of his elders, mothers included, had a hard time arguing with a child trying to further their scholastic ties.

Since Derek could remember, he always found his solace in the seemingly dark recesses of the musty house: beneath the deck outside, his bedroom, the computer room, though his favorite of all was being tucked neatly away within the garage. This was a place where spiders roamed and beetles ruled, with cobwebs that grew to suffocating lengths and all sorts of unsightly pincers and mandibles lurked about, sure to make even the stoniest skin crawl. At least, that's what Derek imagined it to be. He was slightly disappointed when it was not. The first time he finally turned on a real light, he was greeted with just another normal garage.

He opened and closed the garage door slowly, making sure to fill the room up with light long enough to get his surroundings. In the dark, he pawed his way over to his favorite corner and clicked on the little lamp that rested on the floor. The single beam seemed to be stirred by the room itself, the pestering black trying to penetrate the singular light. Derek sat cross-legged, pulling the book out of his bag and resting it within his lap. He swiveled the lamp head around and opened the front cover, again reveling in its beauty. There it sat, a manuscript filled with blank pages and yet still rife with mystery. He leaned in to get a better look. The pages were old, that much was clear, but of what use? He inspected the dust laden rim, the tattered spine, the fading torn and tattered pages, but still nothing. No key, no answer and no real mystery to latch onto. It seemed as if it were just another blank book.

He sighed and sat up, the open book in his lap now angling perfectly towards the light. Derek could feel the heat of his desk lamp in the cold garage as he put his face closer to it, closing his eyes in frustration. What he did not notice was that the closer the book had gotten to the lamp, it too seemed to partake in its heat. Slowly, it began to glow, pulsating as if feeding on the light and heat itself. When Derek opened his eyes, his heart leapt at the sight. He could not help but let his face crack apart into a smile, knowing that he was not crazy. Faintly, ever so slightly, the desk lamp started to fade. As it did, Derek watched the book in front of him pulsate slightly as if it were trying to breath. He shoved the lamp closer, the pages reacting and shining more brightly as he did. No ink was to be found, the pages themselves were still inherently blank, but they now seemed to breathe more regularly. He shoved the lamp closer and closer, the light bulb within it now vibrating slightly as if the very energy was being sucked out of it. The book's glow grew more and more intense, until suddenly the lamp blinked off with a hiss, leaving Derek alone again in the dark. The book's glow began to fade.

Derek wrinkled his nose at the smell of burning rubber. He attempted again and again to turn the lamp back on with a click, but to no avail. The lamp stayed off, the last faint remnants of the glow fading away into nothingness. Irritated, Derek shut the cover. Almost as if in response, the lamp flickered back on. Derek was astonished. He opened the book again, shoving it closer to the now working light and watched the book suck every ounce of light and energy it possessed until the lamp hissed off again. Pleased, Derek sat forward as his heartbeat increased and allowed himself a smile.

"Silliness." The voice broke through the darkness with an accompanying chuckle.

Derek jumped in surprise, desperately trying to will his eyes to adjust to the surrounding darkness. "Who's there?" he asked, squinting. He bounded to one knee, but he could see nothing but the endless pitch black in front of him. He closed the book and held it safely against his chest. The lamp flickered back on.

"Absolute silliness," the voice said with a second chuckle. Derek swiveled the head of the lamp around into the impending darkness, searching frantically for the voice's owner. He sent his makeshift spotlight darting through each patch of darkness and corner in the garage until the lamp eventually found its target.

High above on an abandoned bookshelf, a cat gazed down lazily from its perch. His golden eyes blinked in annoyance as the beam of light hit them.

"Hello, Derek," said the cat. His tail swayed in the air, nonchalant but not without purpose, back and forth in time. It was weird to watch, both slightly soothing and yet still unsettling. Derek could not decide exactly how to describe it. The cat sat forward, resting his head idly on his front paws.

Derek was surprised he did not jump, nor flinch, nor scream at the sight of the talking cat. In fact, his lack of a reaction was ample enough reaction within itself. He just stared incredulously, the book held tightly against his chest. Slowly, his mind started to twist and turn as it tried to figure out exactly who this new cat was. His jaw dropped as it finally clicked. This was clearly the same cat that he watched die only a night prior, only now it was clearly alive and most certainly talking to him. The blood pounded in his ears. This went against every dream, delusion or nightmare he had ever had. He tried to speak, but could not. He tried to wake up, but could not. His tongue was cemented to the top of his mouth. His breathing required more effort than thinking.

"What?" the cat smiled knowingly. "Cat got your tongue?"

Derek scoffed. Not only was it a zombie cat, it was one with a sense of humor. Derek shook himself out of his daze and forced the words out. "You can talk," his voice squeaked. It was the only thing he could think to say.

"Of course I can talk," the cat said, his voice thick with resentment. "Don't be stupid."

"But, you can talk!" Again, it was the only thing Derek could think to say.

The cat looked around the room slowly, unsure of how to respond. "So you've said," the cat replied slowly. He raised an eyebrow.

"Well," Derek fumbled, "you're not allowed to do that."

"And why not?" The cat sat up indignantly.

"Because, cats can't talk!" Derek said, despite himself. "And you're a talking cat!"

"Well, you're a talking human."

"Yeah, but, I'm supposed to talk," he said, slowly questioning the validity of his rights to verbal communication.

"Says who?" the cat asked. He tilted his head slightly in curiosity.

Derek had no answer.

The cat nodded, glancing down at the book. "That's my book you have, Derek."

"How do you know my name?" Derek asked.

"It's written all over your face." The cat flicked his tail. A small shard of glass snapped out of the air, directly in front of Derek's face. Derek peered into the glass warily, directly into his own reflection. Sure enough, *Derek Richard Agons* was etched in perfect cursive across his forehead. He licked his palm and tried to rub it off, which of course only made the cat chuckle again. Another flick of the tail and the shard was gone.

"Now, if that's taken care of," the cat said sitting up, "there's something we need to discuss—"

"—Hold on!" Derek interrupted. "You're dead! I saw you die!"

"Yes," the cat mused, cringing at the memory. "Dreadfully painful thing, dying is."

"So, are you like a zombie?" Derek thought it was an honest enough question. If the cat could talk, it was not farfetched for it to be a zombie.

The cat stared at him as he tried to process the question. "I do not know what that is," he began, unsure whether or not to be offended, "nor do I ever want to be called that again." The cat sniffed dismissively. "I am not dead, I am clearly alive. Nine lives and all that. It comes with the territory." The cat jumped off the bookshelf, landing loosely in front of Derek. "Are you quite finished with the questions? I tire of them."

"What can you expect?" Derek asked as he shrugged and sat back on his hands. "You're a walking dead talking cat. That's like, movie stuff. A boy is going to have questions."

"Be that as it may, you have something that belongs to me." His eyes flickered to the book in Derek's lap.

"I don't think so," Derek said, with a wistful smile. "You can't really steal from a corpse."

"Clever," the cat mused.

"Besides," Derek continued with a shrug, "I'm pretty sure you stole this book from that Prometheus guy in the first place."

"Right, but it was he who stole it from me before that," the cat said with a nod. "I was returning the favor."

Derek chewed on his lip as he surveyed the situation. "So you're saying this is your book then."

"Well, aren't you a quick little boy?" the sat said pleasantly. "It is mine. I wrote it."

Derek laughed and rolled his eyes, leafing through the book's pages. "You're a terrible writer then. The whole thing is blank!"

"You are a silly race," the cat said with a sigh. "Why must you always collectively assume that if you cannot see it or touch it, then it does not exist?"

Derek shrugged. "We're fickle like that."

"A very long time ago, I created that book." The cat's tail slowed in its sway as the cat began to reminisce. "The book before you is at the center of most wars you know of, and some you don't know of at all. People have died for it, empires have fallen because of it, nations have crumbled under it . . . just because of what it can do."

Derek's eyes glistened in the lamplight. "What can it do?" he asked, leaning forward intently.

"It leads people, Derek." The cat looked at the book now, as if enthralled in the beauty of his own work. "It is laced in the knowledge of ages, of sentences that transcend words. It leads people to what they want the most, setting the best course on how to get it. It is not an exact science per se, but it is absolute in its path. Fame, money, love; any sort of tangible or intangible thing you desire." The cat met Derek's gaze, his golden eyes swirling in the glow of the lamp. "You cannot read it yet because you have not quite figured out what exactly that is."

With each of the cat's words, the book seemed to grow heavier in Derek's lap.

The cat licked a paw before setting it on the ground finitely. "I've decided," he said without hesitation. "I would like your help."

"Help?" Derek said, taken aback. He chewed his lip in thought. "With what? I'm not very good at many things."

"Oh, it's a simple task, actually," the cat said. He stretched out his back before turning to Derek with a slight smile.

"I need you to help me kill a dragon."

The garage rang loudly as it was filled with Derek's sudden laughter. He fell on his side, unable to contain himself in face of such an absolutely absurd suggestion. He lay back, trying to contain his breathing. "Yeah, wow," he said as he gathered himself. "That's just not going to happen."

The cat was not amused. "And why not?"

"Because, dragons don't exist," Derek said with a shrug. "And if they did, it's a *dragon*. You don't just kill a dragon."

"A dragon is as much flesh and bones as you or I," the cat scoffed. "They're just a little bigger and slightly meaner."

"You don't get it," Derek laughed again, shaking his head. "Dragons don't exist."

"Just like cats don't talk and books don't magically glow?"

"Yeah," Derek said as the words sunk in. "Exactly like that."

"Well . . ." the cat said, peering into the surrounding darkness. "I'm a talking cat and we both know that book glows."

"Damn," Derek said. He gulped and tried to clear his throat. His could feel his heart pounding in his chest, certain that his brain was actually weighing the possibilities. "You're serious, aren't you?"

The cat nodded. "As serious as death, and we both know I know death."

"Fine, let's say I said yes," Derek shook his head, still trying to process the thought. "Why would I want to kill a dragon in the first place? Dragons are awesome."

"That's very cute, Derek," the cat said with a roll of his eyes, "but this particular dragon wishes to obtain the object resting in your lap and will do everything it takes to get it, no matter how many lives he destroys or families he rips apart. He will obliterate you and everything you have ever known just to have that book back. He will stop at nothing." The cat's eyes sparkled in the lamp light, matching the hue of the glow perfectly. Derek blinked and the cat was now inches away, any hint of playfulness vanished. "That dragon will destroy the world."

Derek looked down the book in his lap in disgust. "He can have it then!" Derek said in earnest, shoving the book forward.

The cat jumped back, shaking his head solemnly. "Were it that easy. Have you not noticed the surge in cataclysmic natural disasters as of late?"

Derek hesitated, his mind wandering back to the news stories from earlier. "Yeah, what about them?"

"They're no disasters, Derek," the cat said, purring sympathetically. "The dragon is ripping apart the world in order to get that book."

"Okay, seriously then, let's give it to him," Derek said offering the book up again. "He can have it!"

"It is not enough." The cat's eyes seemed to sadden then, their golden hue darkening slightly. "I've watched the dragons sit dormant for eons, hiding away as the earth bows down to a lowly race such as humans." The cat sat forward intently. "The dragon has a taste for blood, Derek. I feel as if this book is just an excuse. He will not stop once he has it. Do you remember how I said the book leads? It does not care what the end result is, only that those it takes to are fulfilled in their request." The cat broke eye contact then, weighing each ensuing syllable carefully. "I fear the dragon wants to bring about the end of the world as we know it."

The blood was pounding in Derek's ears. Could the cat hear it? He felt as if the entire world could. "Even if that's true," he said, forcing himself to breathe, "what the hell am I supposed to do about it?"

"Sorry to say, but you are now equipped with knowledge. A true blessing and a curse. Thus, you must do anything and everything you can." The cat's voice dropped to barely a whisper. "Knowing what you now know, could you possibly return to your daily life, a life you hardly enjoy as it is? I've watched you, Derek." Derek's head swirled faintly as he found himself lost in the depths of the cat's golden pupils now inches away from his own. "You are searching for a purpose, for a reason and a rhyme."

The cat leaned in, his back arched at the ready. "And what about your family?" the cat asked softly. "Are you going to be able to go on knowing they are going to die?"

Derek sat up straight, hurt at the mention of his family. "Why can't you do it?"

"Excuse me?" the cat asked. It was not a question he expected.

"If you wrote this thing," Derek said, holding the book out, "then why can't you do it?"

The cat stared at the book, hissing slightly in annoyance. "Knowledge is truly a fickle thing. The book and I don't really get along anymore. Though, it seems that it has taken a liking to you, and that's precisely why I asked." The cat smiled at Derek. "I would not be worried about the why or the how, the book will always take care of it. You just have to have the want."

Derek hesitated, his eyes glued to the book in his lap. "I won't force you to do anything, of course," the cat's voice continued, though Derek's mind barely registered it. "If I did, the book would not respond. It's a choice you'll have to make for yourself.

Derek met the cat's golden stare with his own, in his best attempt at appearing brave. The cat nodded respectfully in response. "You have one week to decide, Derek. One week and one week only. Don't let history say you let the world burn because you were scared."

And just like that, Derek blinked and the cat was gone.

A knock at the door broke the permeating darkness. Derek fumbled to his feet, stuffing the book neatly on a bookshelf, and opened the door to find his mother glaring down at him. "Are you deaf?" she said, putting her hands on her hips. "I've been calling you for the last five minutes. What were you doing down here?"

"Homework," Derek lied again. For once, he wished he actually had been doing homework.

"Well, you have some visitors upstairs," his mother said. She paused in thought to herself, chewing on her lip. "They don't seem very happy."

Derek nodded, throwing the book securely in his backpack and followed his mother out of the garage without a second glance back.

Upstairs, Derek was surprised to find none other than Professor Prometheus and Mr. Everhart awaiting him around the kitchen table, whispering hurriedly back and forth. Mr. Everhart looked his usual self, but Derek was taken aback by Prometheus's attire. The once great and regal man looked absolutely horrible. His once perfectly white hair was tattered and torn across his brow in a gangly mesh of tangles. His eyes were dull now, sinking deep into his once pronounced cheekbones. The professor looked like he had not even remotely considered any sort of hygienic behavior. His beard had started to come in, darker than expected, as it was a more light gray than the perfect white his hair had been.

As the door closed behind Derek and his mom, Prometheus's head swiveled around to meet them. He stood up and darted for Derek, grabbing him around the collar and shaking him violently. "Where is it, boy?" he shouted, his mouth fuming with ferocity. "Where's my book?"

"Calm down, Randall!" said Mr. Everhart, pulling his old friend off of Derek. "We don't want to do anything hasty."

"But he stole it, I know he did!" screamed Prometheus. Mr. Everhart walked Prometheus to a chair, sitting him down. The man's eyes never once left Derek, his glare glued to the teenager's face.

Derek's mother looked to him, her eyebrows raised in question. Derek only shrugged. "I don't know what you're talking about."

"Now Derek," started Mr. Everhart before Prometheus could pounce again. "I saw you with a very old book at school today. Can you at least tell me where you found it?"

"I told you, it's a school book," Derek said with a smile as innocent as he could muster.

"For what class?" asked Prometheus, spewing spittle with each syllable.

Derek hesitated, the words catching in his throat. "Math."

"Liar!" Prometheus screamed again, wrenching himself out of Mr. Everhart's reach. He threw himself at Derek, grabbed him by the shoulders and shook as hard as he could. "Where's my book, boy!?" he screamed, his spit spraying everywhere with vigor. "Give me back my book!"

A hand flew out of nowhere, slapping Prometheus across the face. The old man's skin wrinkled under the blow. "Enough!" shouted Derek's mother, her eyes ablaze in fury. "I will not have you treat my son like this," she yelled as she picked up the phone. "You have exactly three seconds to get the hell off my property or I am calling the cops."

Prometheus only stared at her, his stone cold face a darkened sheet of marble.

"Come on, Randall," Mr. Everhart said softly, grabbing him by the shoulders. The professor loosened his grip on Derek and allowed himself to be quietly led to the door. "We're leaving now, no need for any trouble." Prometheus said not a word, but his eyes never left Derek.

Derek's mother sighed heavily as the door shut behind them. The tension in the room was still palpable, but even she did not know where to start. She stared at her son in desperation. "Do you know what they're talking about?" she asked with another sigh. Her eyes shook with worry.

"No," Derek assured. "I have no idea what they're talking about."

Derek had never seen his mother look so tired.

CHAPTER FOUR

Mr. Everhart was peculiarly absent from school the next day. His replacement was a droll and droopy woman with bags accompanying each orifice of her body. The hair on her arms was as thick as her eyebrows, which were already alarmingly thick to begin with, and Derek could not for the life of him figure out how her body could pour into each crack in her seat. Derek slid himself out from his desk and quietly traversed the classroom, catching a quick glance at the new nameplate that read Mrs. Oswald. "Where's Mr. Everhart?" Derek asked quickly, already wishing he had stayed in his seat.

Mrs. Oswald met his gaze with a beady set of eyes hidden deep within the mountain of skin on her face. "Mr. Everhart will no longer be your teacher." Mrs. Oswald coughed as she spoke, her voice carrying a scratchy quality that just screamed nicotine extracts. "I am the new teacher." Derek quickly retreated back to his desk.

Later that day at lunchtime, Derek sat at his usual spot in the cafeteria. He could not help but glance over to where the girl was the day before. He had almost forgotten about her now, what with the magical talking cats and being accosted by a world-renowned explorer, but in truth he was not exactly sure if it had actually happened. He kicked around the poor excuse for mashed potatoes in front of him absentmindedly. Without thinking, he looked up to where the girl had been the day before, but only scolded himself for being so silly. No one sat at the seat she had occupied. Derek flushed and let the remaining hours and minutes of his school day pass by.

When he finally arrived home, the house was empty. He shouted for his family, but no reply came. The fridge was absent of notes, the kitchen table clean of any location annotations. Derek sat on the couch, placing his bag on the living room table, listening to the complete silence that surrounded him. With such a loud and lively family environment, it was odd to find his house in such complete stillness. He told himself he was being paranoid, and went on with his daily routine.

The second Derek sat back on the couch he was already fighting sleep. He clicked on the television to rot his brain awake, but to no avail. His eyelids were heavy and the couch cushions were more than satisfactory. He placed a hand on his backpack and let the low hum of whatever drivel the television had landed on drift him to sleep.

When he finally woke it was dark outside. He rubbed the sleep from his eyes and the drool from his chin, but it was only after the initial yawn that he noticed the cat sitting on the coffee table. "Hello, Derek," the cat said with a tilt of his head, making Derek jolt in fright. "Have you decided?"

Derek sat up quickly. "Decided?" he said, trying still to rub the sleep from his eyes. "You said I had a week. It's barely been a day!"

The cat shrugged. "Extraneous circumstances have forced your decision."

"Extraneous circumstances?" Derek asked as his stomach began to drop. "What extraneous circumstances? What does that even mean?"

"Those are confidential." The cat's tail swayed steadily.

"Why?"

"Confidential means I'm not going to tell you."

Derek peered at the cat. "So what if I say I won't go?"

The cat chuckled to himself. "With the fate of the world hanging in the balance, I'm not sure you have a much of a choice."

A rustling of leaves broke the ensuing silence. The cat's ears perked up instantly, causing Derek to swivel his head in curiosity. "What was that?" Derek asked, standing up.

"Probably just the wind," the cat replied, trying to sound casual. "Your decision, Derek?" Derek started to walk towards the window. "Your decision please?" the cat said quickly. Derek did not stop. His hand quickly found the window shades. "Derek, I would not open that."

Derek snapped back the shades, peering into the darkness outside. He could not see much. The porch light only covered a rough ten yards in each direction from the bulb and his eyes had not yet adjusted to the darkness, much less to being awake. Still, Derek caught the thin outline of three shapes that melted behind the trees.

"There's something outside!" Derek exclaimed. He turned to the cat. "I saw something outside!"

"And?"

"I think it was a wolf." Derek's brow furrowed in concentration. He did not like the sound of that.

The cat sighed. "Fantastic. Then we have run out of time and you need to make a decision."

Derek sat back down on the couch, bewildered. "Why are there wolves outside? Can they talk like you? Can I talk to them?"

"Derek, I do not have time for silly questions, though I do require your decision."

"Like, dragons, okay, but wolves? Wolves are awesome!" Derek looked to the cat with a smile.

But the cat was not in the mood for playful banter. He was on all fours now, his tail swaying loosely over his head as he sniffed the air. A scent caught the cat's nose. He scoffed. "Time's up." In one fluid motion, his head swiveled around to the kitchen.

Before Derek had time to think, the cat had already leapt over his head. Derek jerked around in time to see the cat land delicately on his front paws in anticipation. From around the corner, Mr. Everhart and Professor Prometheus crept into the kitchen. Prometheus was as filthy as before, though his oddly mismatched beard had filled out more. He wore a dark colored explorer's suit, complete with dark camouflage pants that had more pockets than fabric, and a baggy t-shirt hidden deep beneath a full body coat. Behind him followed Mr. Everhart in his normal teacher attire, slacks and a button up dress shirt, both of which were more ruffled than usual.

Prometheus noticed them first. His eyes went straight to the cat, enraged and confused. "You! How is it possible?" he said incredulously. He shook his head in rage. "I should have known!" Without a second thought, Prometheus lunged for the cat. Poised yet lethal, the cat quickly closed his eyes and then opened them in quick succession, making direct eye contact with Prometheus. Prometheus froze in the air. He was literally stuck there, in both place and posture, perfectly enclosed and unable to move. Derek was beside himself in disbelief, and apparently Prometheus was, too. The old man's eyes widened in a mixture of horror and loathing as he struggled. Prometheus tried his best to move but he was unable to break eye contact with the cat.

"Run, Derek!" the cat yelled. His eyes stayed true to their target. "Grab the book, get in your car and run!"

"But to where?" Derek felt as frozen as Prometheus.

"Don't worry about it, just go!" The cat did not flinch.

"What about you?" Derek urged. His feet were made of stone, his legs unmovable pillars.

"There's no time, Derek." the cat said. "Go!"

Derek grabbed his backpack and jolted, finally forcing his legs to move. He flew past Prometheus, stuck in time.

Mr. Everhart made a grab for him as he passed, but Derek shoved him out of the way with his backpack. He grabbed his keys and wallet from the kitchen counter, shoving them forcefully into his pocket and running to the door.

Somewhere behind him, a window crashed and a wolf landed in his living room, sliding on the shattered glass and rolling quickly up on all fours. A second window crashed as another wolf rolled into the living room. The cat turned and hissed to meet the new threat. His back was hunched, tail as straight as could be. Prometheus fell from the air with a hard thud onto the ground. He groaned and forced himself to his feet with Mr. Everhart's help. The cat looked to Derek for one last fateful second. "Go!" he screamed. Derek turned and ran outside without a second thought. He did not specifically see the two wolves lunge for the cat, but he could hear their growls, the ripping of flesh and the ensuing shrieks of pain.

Derek raced outside, yanking the garage door open. He bolted to his car, already fumbling with his keys. Again and again, he scratched the keyhole, trying to will his hand to be still long enough to unlock his car. He cursed himself under his breath. How hard was it to open a lock?

"That's far enough, boy." A murky and grumbling voice sent chills down his spine. Slowly, Derek turned around to find a monstrous wolf melt into the light from the darkness. His fur looked as if every color had been dripped from its tangled mesh, leaving only a dark and gray compressed mess of tangles behind. The wolf grinned at Derek's displeasure, a single eye glistening in the light of the moon. In place of his other eye was a large scar filled with filth, bile and mangled flesh that never set correctly. "You have something we want," the wolf growled deeply. Two other wolves melted into view behind him. They, too, shared the dark fur coat, but were smaller in both size and stature.

"Just hand it over and no one will get hurt," the one eyed wolf growled.

"Don't be like that, Quinn! Let's play with him a little," the wolf on the left said, inching closer with a maniacal grin. "All they want is the book right?"

"Yeah, Quinn, let's play with him a little," the wolf on the right howled in agreement. He glanced over to the wolf on the left, matching his wolf partner grin for grin. "We don't get out much anymore. Let's have some fun."

"Silence!" spat the one eyed wolf. "We have our orders and that is that." His eye blinked as he turned to Derek. "The book, boy. Don't do anything stupid."

Derek backed into his car, the keys jangling loosely. "What if I don't?"

Quinn smiled. The wolves on his left and right laughed. "Then these two get their wish."

But neither the wolves nor Derek were ready for what came next. From above, a window broke with an alarming crash, sending three bodies flying through its broken remains and out into the open. The bodies twisted and turned in the air, struggling from within for common ground. They hit the pavement with a thud, taking form. Two lifeless wolves now lay deathly silent, a trail of blood spilling from their mouths across the pavement. Derek felt his breath catch in his chest. The third body began to stir. From between the pair of silent wolves, the cat emerged victorious.

"The traitor!" Quinn shouted. "Get him!"

Before the two wolves could move, the cat had already leapt. He landed easily on the first wolf's back, flicked his tail, and hopped off in an instant. As the cat's paws lifted, the wolf erupted in a bold blue flame that seemed to swallow his entire body. Before the second wolf could think, the cat had landed and already jumped off. With a howl, the second wolf erupted in the same blue flame. The cat landed softly in front of Derek, leaving his victims engulfed and writhing. The one eyed wolf growled and he lowered his head to the ready.

With a single nod of thanks to the cat, Derek took a deep breath and steadied his hand long enough to unlock his car. Behind him, he heard the one eyed wolf lunge forward in fury, but the growls and sounds of the ensuing scuffle melted into nothing as he threw his bag down, slammed on the ignition, and peeled out of the driveway. He allowed himself a glance back to where the cat had been, but he could see nothing. His house was already just a blur.

Or it was just a blur until it blew up. The explosion lit up the rear view mirror before it reached Derek's ears. He pulled over, wretched his door open, and observed the ball of blue flame shoot into the night sky. Particles of beam, both metal and wooden, flew through the air before they were snatched up by the fire's all encompassing tentacles. Derek could only assume that his house had just been obliterated. He pulled the car over, jumping out to watch the remains of his house and home dance inside the bale of blue.

"Well, that was a close one."

Derek jolted as the voice came from beside him. On top of the car sat the cat, attending a bloodied forepaw. His tail swished carelessly.

"What the hell just happened to my house!" he screamed, his heart shattering. "My family! What about my family?"

The cat shrugged. "It had to be done. Quinn wouldn't have left me alone otherwise."

"Otherwise?" Derek's arms pounded against the hood of the car. "What the hell happened to my family?"

"Derek, please," the cat said with complete indignation. "Obviously, your family is fine. I made sure to take care of them first."

"Take care?" Derek said, his body shaking uncontrollably. "What the hell do you mean, 'take care?' What did you do with them?"

"I promise, they are safe—"

"—Where are they?!" Derek screamed. He felt as if he was going to throw up.

The cat let Derek exasperate himself as he banged down on the hood of the car. Derek could not help it, for the image of the dust cloud now separating the air where his house had once stood kept playing again and again in his head. He stole a glance. The mythical blue flames finally seemed to subdue, the dust finally settled, and still the cat did not seem to care in the least. Derek watched as the feline just stared at him, his head cocked slightly, his tail swaying, always swaying.

"Are you finished?" the cat asked.

Derek shrugged.

"Derek, I promise you that your family is safe," the cat said with a sigh.

"Right, safe," Derek scoffed, throwing up his hands. "And how are they just magically safe?"

"Look back to your house, Derek," the cat tried to interject.

"Oh, I forgot, the blue flame is for wolves and crazy ass old dudes!" Derek stammered on, flailing his hands with each emphasized word. "It's not like normal humans can actually die in explosions, much less those caused by the blue flame!" Derek huffed, waiting for the cat to interject again, but the cat just sat there, perfectly still and patient.

"Are you finished?" the cat asked again, his brow raised.

Derek panted, the frustration still clear across his face. "For now," he sighed in resolve.

"Good," the cat nodded. "Now, look back at your house."

Derek rolled his eyes and turned reluctantly. Before him, just as it was, stood his house, perfectly intact, not a scorch or flame or brick moved. The entire neighborhood looked as quaint and quiet as it ever did, as if no magical feats or talking animals could ever exist within. It was completely and utterly normal.

Derek felt his heart racing. "How? I don't—"

"The flame is an illusion to distract and ward off anyone who would come looking for you," the cat said, his eyes pinned to Derek's every reaction. "It was for the wolves. Only those I chose saw the illusion, which means I hastily added you in it. It was not on purpose, but I promise, your family is safe." The cat breathed deeply. "Now, I can't fix the broken window or the fact that you'll have disappeared for a while, but your family is sound asleep and they will wake up tomorrow safely in their beds. No one was hurt, no one was harmed, and to the wolves and Prometheus, the house does not even exist anymore." The cat hopped onto the ground, allowing him to sit directly at Derek's feet, peering up. "Think about it, Derek," it purred soothingly. "I did the right thing. You're just going to just have to trust me."

Derek crossed his arms in contempt as his heartbeat finally began to slow. He looked back to his house before rounding on the cat. "But I don't trust you. I don't trust you at all." As he said the words, he still felt his rage subduing. If, at best, he could leave his family safe and unharmed, he knew he could be pleased, he just would not be happy about it.

"Then you must at least try," the cat said.

Derek actually felt his mind being soothed. The realization scared him. He watched as the cat stared at him, his head cocked slightly, his tail still swaying. "So are we done mourning over material things?" the cat asked. "I'd really like to get a move on."

Derek rolled his eyes. "Oh right, the other thing about how you still want me to help you kill a dragon." Derek spat in contempt.

"That is correct."

"You know that's impossible, right?" Derek asked, shaking his head. "I mean, there's no possible way I could even kill a dragon. Ever. Like, ever, ever." Derek threw up his hands in disdain. "It's a dragon! Even if it exists, it's still a dragon!"

The cat turned, hopping back on to the car. "Be that as it may, I feel like this would be an opportune moment to be on our way."

Derek stared. "What? You're not even going to answer my question?"

"Derek, please," the cat sighed, lowering his head in exasperation. "I have been stabbed, clawed, shot, set on fire and even suffocated in the ground as I was encased in cold cement. Half of those things happened in the past week. I have lived and died more times than you can possibly imagine and, logically speaking, that means that I have seen and been through more than you ever will. Why would I waste my time asking you to do something that I felt you could not accomplish?" The cat pawed his way across the hood of the car and crawled into the open window, placing himself in the passenger seat. "Now, I don't like these things you call cars, so the sooner we go, the sooner I can be rid of it."

When Derek did not move, the cat looked at him, his golden gaze begging for rest. "Please?" he sighed. "I'll even add your sugar on top idiom if you must." For the first time, the cat's shoulders actually seemed to slouch.

Derek had lost. He did not know how or why, but he had lost all the same. Somehow, his heart had been soothed and, somehow, his mind was itching at the thought of saving the world. Of course, it was impossible. If there really was such a thing as a dragon that was hell bent on destroying the world, Derek could not fathom in what life he would have a chance against it. And yet, the cat had made a good point. Derek cursed under his breath. The cat always seemed to be making a good point.

"Fine," he said, his face a weak attempt at calmness. "Just don't get your hopes up on the dragon killing part." Reluctantly, he sat himself in the driver's seat and turned the key as he weighed the cat's word. "What now?" he asked, letting the vibrations of the starting car soothe himself.

The cat's golden eyes ignited like gunpowder. "Now," he purred in satisfaction, "we need to get you a weapon."

CHAPTER FIVE

"You have broken our own oaths, wolf. The oaths by which you swore!" Alladin screamed, pointing his little rat paws in objection at Quinn. Abraham watched the wolf blink his singular eye in contempt, offering little resistance. The owl sighed and sat forward impatiently. The council was in turmoil, split decisions across the board, and it needed mending.

"Alladin, you are a guest here," the great gray owl cooed, allowing his own soothing tone to wash over the inner tree canopy. "You have voiced your opinion already and I believe it is high time that you were quiet." Alladin's mouth moved in a silent rage, but he sat down reluctantly. Abraham was thankful for that.

"Now, Quinn," Abraham started, raising a wing to squash any leftover chattering, "as much as I am sure you are enjoying this one-sided interrogation, it is high time we heard your opinion." Abraham gestured, gesturing his wing gently across the open floor. "Step forward, please, and do try to tell the truth."

"Thank you," Quinn said, shooting a snarl toward Alladin. "As I was trying to say, my pack traced the boy back to his house without a problem. I told them to wait till nightfall so as not to arouse the suspicion of any prying eyes." Quinn lowered his head menacingly. "When nightfall broke, we surrounded the house easy enough. I told the pack that this would be routine and simple, as man's security systems are crude and can't even breathe, and sure enough it was. That's when we heard a noise and one of my sniffers picked up a scent of that he had never smelled." Quinn spat. "I should have known then. Imagine, a smell a wolf had never smelled?"

Quinn shook his head and surveyed the council. "I told my wolves to get in there no matter what, and they did, but it wasn't long before another scout picked up the boy's scent outside. I circled around and there he was, backpack in tow, struggling to get into his car. I caught the scent of something terrible and old, a sort of knowledge I had never encountered, coming from his pack and assumed it was the book."

"And where is the book now?" Abraham interrupted. He peered down his beak at Quinn.

Quinn lowered his eyes slightly. "It's wherever the boy is."

Alladin stood furiously. "You mean to say that you, alpha to the scouts, could not apprehend a mere human boy?"

Quinn snarled at Alladin. "We were ambushed from behind."

"And pray tell," the rat said, flashing its gnarled and yellow teeth, "what sort of creature could possibly ambush you?"

"It was the cat."

The council erupted in a flurry of whispers. "Impossible!" screamed Alladin over the noise. Every eye turned to him. "The cat is dead! The owl's told us as much!"

Quinn shook his head. "It doesn't matter what you know to be true, rat! The cat is very much alive. He murdered my two best." Quinn could still see their anguished muzzles writhing wordlessly in the cat's blue flame.

"This is ridiculous!" Alladin yelled again. The council broke out again, this time in more than whispers. Abraham was ready, though, with his wing already lifting. The council quieted.

"Regardless if the cat is alive or not," Abraham said tranquilly, "you have still managed to break our oldest and truest vow; no human shall know we exist." The council murmured their agreement.

"That makes him an outlaw!" Alladin said with an emphatic slam of his tail. His rat brethren slammed down their tails in agreement, egging on their captain.

Abraham looked down solemnly on Alladin. "Are you so quick to banish your brethren?"

Xiu-Fao the panda sat forward, his lumbering body shaking under his weight. "He broke our oath. What choice do we have?" Alladin and his rats greeted Xiu-Fao with their nods of approval.

"Be that as it may," Abraham said, tucking in his wings, "let us remember how few of us remember the old ways. I feel it would be foolish to recklessly abandon fellow brethren because they were forced to make a hard decision. It shall come to a vote."

Quinn sat there with his tail between his legs as the council judged him. Slowly they talked it over, but in the end the result was favorable. The council agreed not to banish Quinn, all accept the few rats and their fellow supporters. Quinn did not care, unable to hide a growl under his breath. To be judged by the great Abraham was one thing, but by rats? His good eye blinked in disgust. He was beginning to see why the cat left the council all those years ago.

Abraham clicked his beak for attention. "Brother wolf, One-Eyed Quinn of the Silver Patch, this council has cleared all allegations forthwith put against you. You are to keep your title, but as punishment, you are alone responsible for our two human prisoners." The great gray owl turned his head upside down in question. "Do you consent?"

"I consent," Quinn growled. He was none too thrilled about being any man's babysitter.

"Good," Abraham said, nodding his head. "Now, we move on to our second matter at hand. Bring in the prisoner."

Quinn watched as the great oak foliage churned away to reveal an opening. He remembered the great old squirrel who had built that mechanism, his bushy tail three times the size of his abnormally small body. "Just a slight bit of cherry honey, oh yes, yes!" the squirrel would say, his head darting off in every direction. "Grown with chestnut and chestnut alike, yes! Only grown where no wind can soil it, yes, then with a twisting hint of the Magellan fruit and next a gate only penetrable by golden fire, yes, yes! And no one had seen golden fire in a thousand years!" The squirrel would laugh to himself then, chattering away as he reminisced about the old times. Quinn saddened. It was a past so few remembered now.

Two hares hopped in slowly, breaking through his memory. They stopped in the middle of the room, their ears fixated inward to the man floating between them. They were brown hares, of the last true-blooded southern tribes; well versed in the knowledge of anti-enormity and wind, as was custom. They carried their prey with ease. The man with the white hair floated forward effortlessly, limbs limping downwards, as if his joints were tied up to a magical unseen castanet.

He looked terrible. His muzzle fur was growing in full now, an odd patch of gray matter that Quinn was unaccustomed to seeing on white haired males. The odd amounts of cloth draped around his person, the clothes that men liked so much to wear, was tattered and torn. He had never been in the cells in the upper foliage and he was sure now he never wanted to.

The hares carried the man to the middle of the council, underneath the great oak canopy. They wrinkled their nose and the man's head slouched before groggily coming to. He looked around at the council, oddly unfazed at what stood before him.

Abraham was first to speak.

"Randall Torrance Prometheus!" said Abraham in his most booming voice, his chest puffing up. The smaller animals, and even some larger ones, could not help but tremble. "You stand now in the presence of the last great council known to this world as the first human in centuries. It is a privilege and an honor for you to be here. Know this before you speak." Quinn bared his teeth in the best smile he knew.

As he came to, the man named Prometheus began to study his surroundings with a poise that should not have existed. His eyes hovered around the room, resting lightly on Quinn, before snapping back to Abraham. Quinn could see the wheels turning in the man's head and he did not think he liked it.

"You come before us a prisoner," continued Abraham, the owl's chest booming with each syllable. "But let it be known that we are not unkind. If you share with us knowledge, we shall share freedom. Likewise, if you share with us nothing, we shall share with you nothing. No nutrients, no liquids, no sunlight, and no freedom. Do you understand this?"

The man cocked his head and laughed long and hard. "Oh, I understand!" A wicked smile broke across Prometheus's face. "Let's see: large owl, old as dirt and deems himself leader of a magical talking animal council. That means you must be Abraham." Prometheus chuckled acidly. "You're even more of a pompous ass than the cat described."

The council broke into a rage. "This is what you bring before us, wolf?" Alladin screamed. "You have disgraced us!" The council added their consent, a new voice breaking in a word of disgust with every passing second. Prometheus stared at Quinn in the midst of the outburst, seeming to study him. Quinn could not help but shudder underneath Prometheus's scrutiny. The man's eyes grew bright as they began to twinkle like a black hole. His lips crackled into a smile.

Again, Prometheus broke into a sharp and piercing laugh, tearing through the jittering crowd noise. The council fell silent. Most seemed shocked and appalled at the very sound. "Now there is a funny sight," Prometheus said, his gaze turning on Alladin. "Rats chastising wolves? I had no idea the mighty wolf was so lowly as to be barked at by vermin!"

Quinn snarled as the council broke into an even more furious anger. He was half ashamed at how true the words rang out, but he could tell his discomfort made Prometheus even more overjoyed.

"You do your worst, bird!" Prometheus screamed over the turmoil. "You are merely a petty circle of cowards who has long since been fading. I have traveled the world through and through, seen dark and terrible things that should not exist, and this is how you try to scare me? With words?" Prometheus yanked back his head and roared with laughter. "I should feather you and put you on a mantel piece where you belong!"

The room grew silent. Every eye was trained on the great owl, waiting in anticipation for Abraham's rebuttal. The great gray owl surveyed his fellow animals and could not help but sigh.

"You are to be pitied, human. You know not what you do." Abraham sat up, his eyes trained on the man. It was not a threat. It was fact. "This is your last chance. Share now, or receive no hope."

"I don't need your hope, owl," the wicked man said as he broke off into another cackle. His laughter roared and roared, the noise seeming to absorb into every limb of the foliage auditorium as if no other sound existed.

"Shut him up!" roared Xiu-Fao. The hares looked at each other, then to Abraham who nodded gravely. They closed their eyes and locked their ears in unison on Prometheus's face, sending it retching backwards in a deep sleep until he finally laughed no more.

"And you say we should let the wolf stay, Abraham?" Alladin fumed. "Even after this?" The council raged in a tumultuous chatter.

"Maybe we should cast another vote?" Pathos the panther growled, sitting forward into the light. Abraham noticed that Pathos had been oddly silent throughout the ordeal, but was not shocked to find she wanted another vote. She was always one for democracy and discipline. Quickly the council agreed as shouts of "Banish the wolf!" began to arise. Quinn snarled then at Alladin, meeting the rat's twisted smile with his own good eye. The rat did not so much as flinch. In fact, he seemed to revel in the chaos.

Maybe the wicked man was right.

"Enough!" Abraham bellowed, standing for the first time in a hundred years. He stretched his wings their full fourteen feet and for a second it seemed like a second moon had risen in the room. "It has been decided!" Abraham looked down upon Alladin, who shrunk under the colossal beauty of the great gray owl. "You shall be silent, rat. Know your place." Alladin shrunk into his makeshift seat. Abraham clicked his beak impatiently, lowering himself back down to his roost. He felt his bones creak and strain underneath him and he cursed his sudden outburst. They were all growing old and him the oldest. "Good," he said quietly, collecting his thoughts and bobbing his head back and forth in age. "Now, we shall press on to other matters."

The wolf named Quinn observed silently as the council brought in the second human prisoner, an Adrian Gilder Everhart. This second man turned out to be much more of a help, but Quinn could not help but glance to where Alladin sat. The greedy little vermin twisted his hands in delight with his fellow pack as they voiced their constant opinions. Quinn was disgusted by them. Yes, Alladin was the prince of a great nation of rat kind over in Egypt, thus gaining himself a right to sit as a guest on the highest of councils, but Quinn could not quite help but feel a slight twang at his pride, for of course Alladin was still only a rat.

It was then that Quinn could not help but chuckle to himself. For the first time, he realized that no wolf sat on the greatest and oldest of councils the world had ever known.

CHAPTER SIX

"What if I freeze it and *then* set it on fire?" the cat said, his head cocked in a curious fashion.

Derek sighed and slammed the hood of his car closed. "For the last time," he said, tired of answering stupid questions, "I really doubt any of your super cat magic is going help. It's a car engine. It's not alive. You can't just burn it and be done with it."

"A pity," the cat said, his eyes squinting. He looked positively confused. "If it does not breathe, then why would you trust it?"

Derek threw up his hands. "It's a car!" he said, rolling his eyes. "You're not its best friend, you don't establish a bond. It just takes you places."

Derek sat on the ground and surveyed the desolate dirt road the cat had set them on. They had driven a good two days out from any real civilization or gas station. Thickly rooted trees surrounded the poor excuse of a street he sat on, expanding in each direction as far as the eye could see. The sky above was a very boring blue with no cloud coverage to shield the beaming sun or the lack of fresh air. Derek sighed and almost wished that it would start raining gasoline. In his mind, he had already begun to experience weirder things as of late, so why not?

He knew he was an idiot for thinking the cat could actually fill his gas tank up with magic. He had asked repeatedly, making sure the cat knew what he was doing, but the end result was a burnt carburetor and no tools to even begin fixing it. Not that Derek would have known where to begin. In truth, he knew very little about cars in general. As the smoke rose after the fire was finally out, the cat had just shrugged and sat, patiently licking his forepaw.

"Well, that is more than enough pouting for one day," the cat said decidedly. "Shall we be on our way?" The cat's eyes seemed to glisten more than usual.

"And where will we be going without a car?" Derek asked, though he did not really care about the answer.

"I told you already, Derek," the cat said, peering deep within the woods. "We need to get you a weapon."

Derek nodded apathetically. "Right, a weapon," he said, resting his head in his hands. "And what kind of weapon can kill a dragon, exactly? Is it some sort of fiery sword that steals the soul of whoever it touches? Maybe an axe that can cut through any material? How about a staff that triples your experience points and lets you level up that much faster? That's just what I need." Derek laughed to himself mockingly. "Because I really don't think I'm at a high enough level for dragon slaying."

The cat just stared. "Are you finished?"

Derek sighed. Again. "Yeah, fine." He stood and brushed himself off. "Let's just do whatever you want to do."

"Good, because we're actually here," the cat said, starting his descent into the woods. "Funny how that works, isn't it? Follow me then."

Derek raised an eyebrow. "Wait a second," he said, looking back at his car. The smoke had subsided, though the stench was still prevalent. "Did you burn my car on purpose?"

The cat did not respond, though the way its tail perked up at the thought was more answer than Derek could take. He huffed and grumbled to himself under his breath, but the cat was disappearing into the woods now so he followed nonetheless. The leaves crunched noisily underfoot as they gave way to Derek's muddied tennis shoes. It was interesting noise, but only made more so when Derek compared it to how the cat's deft paws made no sound at all.

The snapping of branches on the dirty forest floor became like a ticking clock in Derek's head, each step keeping time within itself. By now, Derek could have sworn it should have been nighttime, but still the sun peered relentlessly through the trees. Why did all the trees look the same? Derek could not tell if the wood was growing thicker or if the ground was getting thinner. He looked over his shoulder. He was not even certain that they had been walking in a straight line. Normally, Derek would have chalked up another lost woods outing to his terrible sense of direction, but these woods were eerie. He looked around them, peering off into the distance with each step. He could not help but shudder. These woods felt wrong somehow.

"Where are we going exactly?" Derek asked to break the silence. He was not fond of the silence.

"Where we are going is where I lead," the cat said simply. He stopped and observed the woods carefully, scanning the trees as if trying to jog his memory. He lifted a leaf and licked the bottom. "If that is a problem, then please feel free to turn around at any point and drive your car back home." The cat chuckled to himself.

"You know, I don't find that funny in the least," Derek said, observing the woods. "You're the one who continually destroys my life and expects me to deal with it."

"I have not destroyed your life," the cat said absentmindedly. "It's just that circumstances present themselves with challenges that I try to fix." The cat shrugged. "I will never understand the human appreciation for cold metal." The cat continued walking. Derek followed behind.

"So, should we worry about any squirrel or birds we might see?" Derek he walked in single file with the cat. He had been keeping an eye out, but for some reason no animals seemed to live in these woods.

"No."

"Why not?" Derek asked, looking around.

"Because I said so."

Derek thought for a second. "Well, how do we know there aren't evil talking animals who want to gnaw our eyes out?"

"Because, obviously, eyes aren't that appetizing."

"But what if they tried to anyway?"

"Your eyes have nothing to worry about. Besides, they'd go straight for your throat. Human jugular has a very pleasant texture."

Derek's eyes widened. "You've tried it?"

"Derek," the cat sighed, "if I had known you were going to ask so many questions, I wouldn't have asked you to come along." He stopped at a broken tree and slid a claw from his paw. With a single swipe, he scratched off a piece of bark and nodded to himself knowingly.

Derek chewed his lip, unable to shake the thought. "So . . . do we or do we not have to worry about evil talking animals?"

"Not." The cat stepped forward and arched his back, his tail shooting straight up like an arrow. With the blink of an eye, the broken tree lifted into the air, splitting in half with a crack. Dark maple began to seep out of its timber innards in every direction.

"What's happening?" Derek asked nervously.

"Just watch," the cat said quietly.

The tree hovered in place, the maple oozing onto the ground. Slowly, the dusty forest floor soaked up the seeping syrup, breathing deeply. An odd assortment of vines and shrubbery, intertwined with flowers that were as vibrant as they were mismatched, sprang forth from the once barren ground in every direction. In a frenzy, the once split tree burst into a hundred different pieces with a crack as it shattered from the core. A million shards of bark shot into the sprouting vines, intertwining themselves in a large, cube like shape. Derek watched breathlessly as the magic shrubbery settled itself in the shape of a modestly sized house, complete with chimney.

The cat walked forward without a second thought as the door swung open.

Derek didn't move. "What is it?" he asked.

The cat rolled his eyes. "It's a house. Don't tell me you've forgotten them already?"

"Of course not," Derek said, examining the outside. There was a wider assortment of flowers on its walls than Derek had dreamed existed. "Is it your house?"

The cat scoffed. "Why would I need a house?"

"Well whose is it then?" Derek plucked one of the flowers. A second, different colored flower with sharp thorns and a wide mouth grew back in its place.

The cat's golden eyes were the only color that stood out more against the surrounding foliage. "This house belongs to none other than Professor Prometheus."

"He can use magic?"

"Don't be stupid," the cat said, walking inside. "He built the house with his own limited fingers, though I guess it was a more modest looking log cabin last time he saw it. I just hid it from him."

"Wouldn't he still know where it was?" Derek followed inside.

"No. Outside of the fact that he'd never think his house would remain hidden in a broken tree, I used some added precaution. Remember, home is where the heart is,

Derek. I just happen to know a spell from a previous life that takes that suggestion literally."

Peculiarly enough, the house from the inside was vastly different, appearing just to be a modestly crafted wooden hut. Its furniture placement was meticulous in shape and form, chopped from the same tree as the inside walls, which were each decorated with paintings and engravings in languages that Derek did not know existed and lined with odd shaped trinkets that looked to serve no real purpose. There was a moderate sink, a well enough sized cot mixed in with some very odd looking furniture, but the strangest thing was the fireplace. Stonemason rock, cut thickly and neatly over a brazen hearth that burned continuously. Derek could not help but wonder why someone could ever think to light a fire in a wooden house.

"So, where's my weapon?" Derek asked, beginning his search through the surrounding stacks of old parchment and hand crafted boxes. "I didn't know Prometheus owned a fire-sword-axe-spear of magical death."

"Here it is, Derek," the cat said, hopping up onto the fireplace and stopping next to a wooden plaque. Resting peacefully in the middle of the plaque was a neatly ordained, hand crafted revolver.

"A gun?" Derek said, incredulously. "My magical dragon slaying weapon is a *gun?*" He could not scoff, crossing his arms in disgust.

"Yes," the cat nodded. "Is there a problem?"

"Of course there's a problem, it's a *gun.*" Derek waved his hands in contempt. "There's no way you can kill a dragon with a gun."

The cat tilted his head. "And why not? Do guns not kill things?"

"Sure, they kill things, but not a dragon!" Derek shrugged. "It just feels wrong."

The cat stared blankly. "Would it help if I told you that it's a magical gun?"

"Yes." Derek nodded to himself. "Yes, it would. Is it a magical gun?"

"No." The cat did not even hesitate.

"Then no, don't tell me it's a magical gun because that would be a lie."

"I don't see what the big problem is, Derek," the cat said, his tail beginning to sway. "Many guns throughout the ages have proven themselves able to kill many a thing, and this one did a fine enough job with me." The cat looked at the cold revolver warmly. "Here, take it. Try it out."

Derek walked to the hearth and pulled the gun off the plaque. "It's just cold steel. It doesn't feel right. It shouldn't be able to kill a dragon."

"And what is a sword but cold steel?"

"I guess, but it'd be cooler if it was on fire or something."

The cat's eyes narrowed. "Derek, if it were on fire, then you couldn't hold it."

Derek took a seat at the table, placing the gun in front of him and cracked his neck in frustration. He stared at the gun, trying his hardest to be interested, but he was still thoroughly disappointed. The cat jumped onto the table, lying on his side.

"If it helps, it does shoot flaming bullets," said the cat, licking his paws.

"Really?" Derek perked up. Flaming bullets. He liked the sound of that.

"Well, no, but they'll make your flesh feel like it's on fire," the cat quipped. "I know."

"How?" Derek asked, curious again. Being a teenager, his interest was easily grabbed.

"I was shot, of course," the cat said, examining the gun with Derek. "In fact, I was shot by that very gun. Prometheus used it to kill me."

Derek stared at the gun with a newfound liking for it.

"That should not make you so pleased," the cat said coolly.

Derek picked up the gun then, his mind already wandering. He let the weight of it shift in his hand, moving it deftly from side to side. He was surprised to find he rather liked the feel of the solid steel surrounding the hilt cover, but he did not like admitting it for it was still a gun, utterly unromantic. No real dragon would let himself be killed by a gun, Derek knew. Still, the longer he held it, the braver he began to feel. As he peered into the engravings surrounding the back hatch twisting meticulously up to the hammer, Derek could feel the gun warming up to him. The handle felt warmer, as if it were just another part of his hand. Without thinking, he clicked off the safety and cocked back the hammer, peering down the nose of the worn down revolver. Deftly he picked a spot on the wall and pulled the trigger. Nothing happened. Derek was perturbed. He wanted, no, he needed to hear the roar of a bullet escaping the chamber, ripping into the wall exactly where he wanted. He cocked back the hammer a second time, firing again, this time at a plate. Still nothing. Was it not loaded? He felt like screaming. Why was it not working?

In his haste, Derek failed to notice the steady flow of the cat's tail and the feline's perfect breathing. The cat stared at the back of Derek's head, his eyes focused. Not that it would have helped the poor boy. The cat was too careful for that.

Derek slammed the gun down on the table. "Interesting piece of work, isn't it?" the cat said with a grin. Derek stared at the gun, his hand trembling. He thought he could still feel the burning in his palm from the handle.

"What was that?" Derek said at last. "What just happened?"

The cat paced over to the gun, his smirk a novelty in the wood cabin. "That gun is a very evil thing. It is no ordinary metal. I have no idea how Prometheus came to be its owner, but he seems to have misshapen it somehow into the evil twisted thing before you. It's a perfect match for the one whom it armed." The cat rested his ear lightly upon the gun. "You can hear its heartbeat if you listen close enough," the cat said warily. "Such an evil thing."

Derek stared. "But the Professor was so nice when I first met him."

"I'm sure he was," the cat scoffed. "He's more of a fake than anything. Did you know he had his hair permanently turned white so he'd have the old grandpa appearance? He's actually the same age as your academic teacher."

"He and Mr. Everhart are the same age?" Derek asked.

"They grew up together as I understand it. Both decided to teach, one in high school, the other fancied being a professor. Of course, then he fancied himself a great explorer, though everything he's ever discovered or done has been for his own benefit. Who knows if even half of his stories are true." The cat walked back to his original spot on the table's edge. His tail began to tick back and forth in its usual fashion.

Derek pushed the gun away from him. "Why would I want to use something evil?"

"The fact that you want nothing to do with that weapon is the exact reason it must be you using it," the cat said knowingly. "It's simple. We get you to the dragon and the gun does the rest itself."

"Yeah, because killing a dragon is so simple." Derek sat back exasperated. "Where does this dragon live exactly? It doesn't seem like a dragon is that easy to hide."

"You'd be surprised. This particular dragon is quite ingenious in his surroundings."

"How did you find him the first time?"

"Well, the dragon's whereabouts weren't exactly a secret," the cat said, arching his back. "All knowledge leaves a trace, or a certain smell, like a taste in the air that is tangible. It has weight and with weight comes a trail. I've just always had an innate sense for it." The cat smiled wickedly. "The council has control issues. They used to love making sure they knew exactly where every animal who still remembered was. Their location, what they were doing and who they were still talking to."

Derek sat forward. "What do you mean, used to?"

"Well, they used to until I left. I was their premier tracker."

"You were on the council?" Derek asked, perplexed. "I thought you hated the council."

"Hate is a very strong word, though there are parts of me that probably do," the cat said offhandedly. "We just have very different views on how to live. The council likes to think they are superior, and in their superiority they alienate themselves from reality. I just prefer to do my own thing."

Derek laughed. "So you want to fight with wolves, kill dragons, pretend to blow up houses and ruin car engines without a bunch of crotchety old animals breathing down your neck?"

The cat nodded. Its tail seemed to nod in unison. "There are many things the council and I disagree upon." He peered out the window in thought, his eyes stretching out beyond the bright woods. After a moment, the cat looked back to Derek. "And now we move. Are you ready?" It was most unsettling.

"I guess so," Derek said, trying to see outside into the day. He could only catch a glance of treetops and clouds through the odd light beams of the playful sun.

The cat walked outside, not waiting for any sort of reply. He did like to be punctual to his own clock. "Don't forget the gun, Derek," the cat said on his way out. Hesitantly, Derek opened his bag and placed it at the edge of the table. He took a book from the bookshelf and scooted the gun into his bag, not wanting to touch it. He was not very fond of evil things.

After three more days of walking, Derek awoke to a dark and murky sky muddied with dirty little clouds and veiled visibility. Derek was confused at the nightfall, not too sure when he had fallen asleep, but based on his experiences over the past few days he made the wiser choice not to question it. The cat sat on top of a withering tree stump that Derek did not remember being there, his tail swaying. Derek wondered if the cat ever stopped counting time in his head or if it was a natural occurrence. The cat sat intently, waiting for someone or something to break through the black night that was suffocating the trees.

The cat looked back at Derek. "I can promise that what you are about to see is going to frighten you," the cat said. Derek did not like the sound of that. "Regardless," the cat continued, "I am going to need you to remain calm. You must remember that it is not real, but instead a very powerful illusion."

"Wait, what?" Derek asked wearily, trying to rub the sleep from his eyes. He stood uneasily. He was not too fond of where this was going. "What is happening?"

"I don't actually know," the cat said offhandedly, "but I can promise it will be most uncomfortable. Dragons do not usually enjoy being disturbed."

"Dragon? Are we going to the dragon? Why can't you just take me to him?"

"It seems he has the ability to shield me from his whereabouts," the cat sighed. He lowered his head in agitation. The cat did not take too kindly to being outsmarted. "Wherever it is implanted in my head that the dragon lives, it seems that I cannot return to it. Makes sense, after the last time I was there." The cat sniffed dismissively. "When I first recovered from the bullet wound your Professor Prometheus inflicted, I tried retracing my steps to the dragon's lair only to find it did not exist. In its place lingered the scent of some very powerful daydream, akin to the death of a rose." The cat peered into the woods, his eyes gazing deeply on nothing in particular. "Most unpleasant smell to be sure, yet still slightly fulfilling. It was the first knowledge I've encountered in a long time that I could not unravel." The cat looked to the boy now hanging on his every word. "I wandered for what must have been weeks, though in truth I forgot any sense of time. These woods seem innately crafted with such a thing in mind. I tried everything I knew, but to no avail. It had been so long since something stumped me, I . . ." He smiled sympathetically. "I'm sorry, I was rambling. Please, lay the book out in front of you Derek."

"I just woke up," Derek said groggily. He unruffled his shirt and threw away the rock that had been jutting into his back. "Can I please have a second to—"

"Derek, you know I don't like being interrupted."

"Yeah, but –"

"Derek. The book?"

Derek grumbled, yet still complied, dipping into his backpack and withdrawing the book. It still surprised him how old the book seemed to be, though taking into account how long the cat said the book had lived Derek was even more surprised that it had not yet crumbled into dust. He knelt and placed it on the ground.

"Open it and stand back," the cat said, his golden eyes transfixed. Derek complied warily.

"Now, this next part is very important, so I need you to listen and just do as I say. I don't need a long-winded question expecting answers that I don't have. Whatever happens, you need to go with it. Understand?"

Derek stared back blankly. "No, I can't say that I do." His palms were beginning to sweat.

"Try to be still, Derek." The cat stiffened his tail. "This is where the fun begins."

Bit by bit, the cat's tail began to sway to a slow and steady beat. Left to right, left to right. The cat closed his eyes and began to fill his lungs with air. Just when Derek was almost sure that he was going to suck everything breathable out of the surrounding area, the cat's eyelids began to glow. His head jerked up, his eyes bursting open like signal beams as light overflowed from his eye sockets, splitting the treetops with their luminance. Derek shielded his face and could not help but cower. He peered through his fingers just long enough to see the cat open his jaw wide and let a small ball of light lift into the air. It escaped the cat's throat with a rushing sensation, finding a nice spot to hover in the air over their heads. The ball of light was hot and furious, glowing like a miniature sun. As Derek's eyes adjusted, a deep and uncontrollably shudder ran through the cat's body. "Don't worry about me, Derek," the cat said wearily. He looked exhausted. His chest lifted heavily as if a boulder was on his shoulders. Behind him, his tail swayed just enough to keep his heartbeat decreased. "Keep your eyes on the book!"

The book hovered in mid air now, basking in the radiance of the mini sun. Every tear, rip, page, crease and fold of the book seemed to pulse energetically. Tendrils of light began to siphon off from the orb as they were sucked directly into the book's depths. Derek felt a shiver travel through his body, now sharing in the book's newfound warmth. He smiled genuinely, his eyes beginning to sting with tears. He felt happy for the book, so very happy. He wished he could absorb the light from the dangling mini sun the way the book did. It was so effortless. He felt a pang of jealousy, standing there alone, as the book was filled with life. His eyelids lifted in step with its pulsating. He knew then that he could not look away, not that he would in the first place. In fact, he had no idea why he would ever think about looking away at all. It was such a silly notion; the book was far too beautiful. Nothing could ever be as fantastic as the floating book in front of him was in that moment. But then Derek knew he *had* to look away. He needed to. In fact, nothing would make him happier than to turn on his heel and stare longingly into the dark and shadowy woods.

So he did. He lifted his hand, shielding the rays from the burning globe, and patiently let his eyes focus on the dark of the forest. Off in the distance, two glowing lights flickered on and off. That was odd. He squinted, trying to make out the shapes. They floated like little lamps, illuminating bark and oddly shaped leaves that hung on by a thread. They grew closer, pulsating bigger and brighter. Derek smiled. He felt as if he had been made for this exact moment in life. He lifted his hands in waiting for the two little floating lamps in the distance. They drifted over to him and landed softly in his palms. Their tiny feet sent the most wonderful prickling sensations tingling through his skin. It felt as if blood had finally started to flow within his veins.

"Do you see? Do you see?!" he laughed as the little orbs crawled around his hands. "Fireflies. They're fireflies!" The tiny bugs flicked their wings, letting the light from their abdomens breathe. Derek watched in jubilation as the two little lamps crawled up his wrists, making molecular footsteps and tripping over his arm hairs.

From his new perch in the treetops overhead, the cat did not see. For him, the woods stood dark and motionless, the light now completely absorbed by the glowing book and Derek staring stupidly into it. There were no fireflies, nothing to be so excited about, just a boy staring into an ancient glowing book. The cat bared his fangs, hissing slightly. This display of knowledge was more powerful than he had expected. The cat knew then he could not control it and thus he did not like it.

Derek felt a tickle at his ear as a firefly landed on it. His chin twitched under the soft patter of another one's foot. Derek went along with it, sure that this was exactly what must be done. He cringed initially as the first firefly crawled its way into his ear, but he choked the irritation down immediately. This happiness would soon be over and he wanted it to last forever. The second bug made its way through his outer earlobe. Derek breathed. It was over. Derek's eyelids flickered open. In the dark woods ahead, fireflies were perched on the trees in a single line, making a makeshift path.

In the distance, right on the edge where peripheral meets perception, stood a woman. Her stark white linen dress flowed gingerly down her body, starting at the dark curls of hair flowing down to her shoulders. Her bare toes scrunched, taking in the grass around them. A smile broke her lips as she sighed and stretched, catching Derek's eye with a twirl of her dress. Derek knew this girl; he had seen her before. What was this magic? Who was she? Derek tried to remember what it was to feel astonished or confused, but in truth the emotions escaped him.

With a flick of her wrist, she offered a single finger over her lips as if shushing him. Derek knew what she meant. He was not to think, he was to follow. She turned on her heel and headed down the firefly path. Without a moment's hesitation and with an honest yearning for what truly mattered, Derek straightened his backpack, picked up the book in his arms, and followed. He did not speak. He did not look back. He just followed.

The cat's lips eased into a wary smile. At least the book was doing what it was supposed to be doing. The cat may not be happy with the odd scent the book gave off, but he could at least shield himself from it. That much the cat knew. Derek began to make his way through the trees and the cat jumped from branch to branch, keeping in step. The woods were dank and dark, all but indiscernible except for a pair of golden eyes, a pulsing glow and the sound of crunching leaves. The cat made sure to keep his distance just enough so that whatever secrets the book held, it would never know his presence or the secrets he carried himself.

CHAPTER SEVEN

"You don't have to put up such a fight, you know. It's not like they're trying to kill us or anything." Mr. Everhart tore off another round of berries from the stems now growing out of their foliage built cell, a coiling mass of thorns and flowers, barely big enough to fit the two human prisoners. He bit down gingerly, breaking through the leather skin to the slightly unnerving gooey center, his favorite part. Every time the goo touched his tongue, his mouth exploded with an aroma of freshly picked strawberries. Freshly picked strawberries were his favorite.

Mr. Everhart stretched his back, leaning against the tightly entwined vine wall of the cell as a brush of flowers sprouted quickly to cushion him. If he were one for guessing, he would have placed their cell somewhere in the upper foliage of the mammoth tree they were being held in. He did not remember the night of their capture per se, only the bits and pieces before and after. He remembered Randall's loose explanation of a talking cat and a glowing book that granted wishes or helped you achieve whatever you wanted most or some lunacy. Then, he remembered trying to drag Randall's limp body from the house when it suddenly erupted in a tower of blue flame. He remembered seeing Derek's house stand completely still in that flame, unscathed and untouched, though the second he had looked up it seemed as if the house had exploded into tiny bits. He remembered not understanding.

And then he remembered his only thought. *Magic.*

Next thing he knew, he awoke floating in the air as a mass of rabbits circled him, their every movement twitching in unison. He could not move a single muscle and could only barely string together a coherent thought. He remembered the dank smell of trees and moss and the slivers of light breaking through the thick tree line overhead as he caught a glimpse of wolves and a second encirclement of hares and their own floating personnel. He did not know how long he had spent floating literally and figuratively out of consciousness, but he did remember the guttural sounds of English escaping what looked like a panther's mouth. That's when he remembered he had thought he had died and been reincarnated, or had just gone completely insane, whichever came first. The next thing he knew he awoke in his foliage prison, Randall sitting unmovable and silent across from him. Really though, it was not half as bad as Mr. Everhart originally thought. When he had been taken in front of the talking animals and what seemed to be their leaders, they were rather nice, all things considered.

He sighed peacefully, leaning his head against a freshly sprouted pillow of flowers and lifting his hand to the ceiling. The vines overhead unraveled and sprouted into a fresh batch of berries. At first he had been skeptical, but his hunger drove him to feed. He plopped another of the berries in his mouth and let the rare little bundle of exotic juices explode in merriment. "Starving yourself isn't going to solve anything, Randall," he said, chewing gingerly. "You look like a skeleton more and more every day."

On the other side of the cell, Prometheus sat calmly in front of the only opening the dank plants offered; a twisted group of thorny weeds spread just enough for

Prometheus to catch faint glimpses of the scurrying shadows outside. He stiffened his back, allowing the air to flow smoothly through his nostrils, keeping his arms and legs crossed, trying to take up as little space as possible. This was by no means an offering of comfort to the inferior man lazily gorging himself across the cell, but rather a way to assess the situation. His nose twitched. The smell of what could only be another batch of berries for Everhart to gorge himself on burned his nostrils, sending them twitching in annoyance. Prometheus added flowers and berries to his mental list of things he hated.

Captured. The word caught in his chest, stuck there as if impaled by a ragged and twisting knife. It was his complete lack of composure that got him into this mess. He should have known that a bullet would never be enough to stop that damned cat. He should have expected the feline fiend's untimely return. Instead, he was now sharing a frilly prison with a complete dolt, being interrogated by vermin and lesser species that thought too highly of themselves. He straightened his back again, making sure to let the tension release from his shoulders. There was little sense in losing his cool twice in a week. He would be ready for whatever came.

Yet, it was probably true, he reflected to himself, thinking about how brutish his appearance had probably become. Ever since their capture, he could feel his once neatly trimmed beard tickling long below his shoulders. His hair grew in step, matching his beard for length and an increasingly wiry intensity with each new hour of added sweat and grease. For the life of him, he could not tell if he could now see his own gaunt eye sockets or if it was just the growing number of bags collecting under them. He offered himself a slight smile. He was probably thin enough to pass himself off as a walking skeleton if his gangly fingers were any indication.

He looked out through the twisting thorn cell door he had positioned himself in front of, staring blankly in thought. The ever-crawling thicket of thorns began to relax him with their monotonous upward movement. He looked over his shoulder at Everhart preoccupied with a new fruit now growing from underneath him and scoffed. He turned back to his cell door and studied it from end to feasible end. It was less of a door and more of an opening covered in an ever-growing, thorny testimonial to the one thing in this life he had absolutely no taste for. *Magic.* He wanted to spit at the thought, but he did not feel like expending the energy. So, Prometheus sat and stared, letting the wheels churn in his head.

Then again . . .

A plan was beginning to formulate.

That night, Prometheus stood over Everhart, watching him sleep. It was odd how peaceful he looked, though it was even odder how quickly the man could pass out. So deep and unaware and uncaring, and every night had been the same. Like clockwork, whether or not Everhart was deep in thought or babbling on about some new obsession, the man would pass out at the same time, every time. After what felt like a week, Prometheus began to notice it. Now he knew it was happening, but he also knew that he had to be sure.

And so, he knelt over his sleeping friend, grabbed him by the collar and slapped him across the face. He counted to fifty in his head, waiting patiently. Mr. Everhart made absolutely no reaction, not a single stir of motion. Prometheus placed a finger under Everhart's nose only to find the man was still breathing. Interesting. Prometheus lifted his hand again, this time letting fly a grueling full handed slap that landed squarely across Everhart's jaw. The sound of impact was almost sickening. Almost. Regardless, his friend Mr. Everhart barely stirred. Prometheus reached down and checked his friend's pulse, still beating regularly. Prometheus nodded to himself, satisfied. He could not help but wonder at exactly what were in those berries.

Three nights later, he readied himself, knowing his next plan of attack. He knelt at the cell door and took off his shirt, ripping both sleeves off of his once gentlemanly attire. He placed both strips of cloth across themselves on the foliage floor in front of him, directly next to the thorns, and rested his hands on top of them.

As expected, the thorns grew furiously thicker the closer his hands got to them. He could not tell what exactly caused the reaction, just that the thorns themselves seemed to detect him. They did not move for the cloth or any other object, just him and Mr. Everhart.

He placed his palms out in front of him, scandalously close to the thorn door, and waited for the thorns to gather as thick as possible as they twisted in a gnarled, spiky shield, until finally pulling his hands back and off the cloth. As he originally surmised, the thorns digressed, sensing no apparent danger from just the cloth itself. For the first time in a long time, Prometheus allowed himself a genuine smile. He lashed out and started yanking handful by bloody handful.

Mr. Everhart could not say exactly how much time had passed when the shrill sound of a bird's shriek came ripping into their cell. All he knew was that he felt like he had slept longer than he had ever been awake. Yawning, he rubbed the sleep from his eyes, attempting to sit up. His head felt heavier than he had ever remembered. He sat forward, planting his face in his hands. He flexed his jaw groggily. With the second, or maybe third or fourth shriek of the bird, he jerked his head back in shock.

"Whatever that is," he said, massaging his forehead, "I would really like it to stop." He pulled himself upright and gathered in his surroundings. "Randall, what in the world is going on?" he said, finally turning toward the front of the cell. Everhart's breath caught in his throat. Prometheus sat still as stone in the exact position Everhart had left him in, but now his shirt was completely missing, revealing a back littered with aged scars stretched out in every direction over a surprisingly taught and muscular figure.

What really alarmed Everhart, though, were Prometheus's arms. Crossed against his chest, they were now covered in what looked like a thousand fresh and bloodied gashes and tears from shoulder to wrist. Though a few of the scratches were unthreatening, and most had seemed to just draw blood, it was the deeper gashes that were most disconcerting. He was confused how they ever coagulated at all based on how fresh they looked. What was more, underneath Prometheus's crossed arms Everhart could see his hands, covered in the bloodied scraps of what was left of his shirt.

"Randall," he said, fumbling to his knees. "What the hell happened? You look like you were tortured!"

Yet Prometheus's only reply was a contemptuous scoff. A man who sleeps like a princess on his newly sprouted bed of flowers did not elicit a response.

Everhart kept asking questions, though Prometheus tuned him out without any real effort. Through the mist outside their cage, he could see faint shapes of random animals finally starting to emerge, fluttering and scurrying around in haste. Quickly, he clenched each muscle in his body in unison and counted to ten. Then, he let himself relax completely, staring blankly into the vine laced hallway. He was waiting for what he knew not and he smelled of blood. His head bobbed slightly in approval.

Three rats dropped down from the treetops above in perfect harmony. They landed in front of the cage in a triangle formation. The two in front had their paws raised; their every movement was perfectly synchronized. They twitched their scraggly tails together, their heads darted right to left, and their paws drew symmetrical squares in the air together. The third rat was at the thorn door, his teeth jittering and paws drawing a triangle shape over a small section of the door. Prometheus watched the vermin intently.

Everhart began to crack then, yelling with increasingly more fervor, but Prometheus kept ignoring him. Honestly, it was quite easy to do. Without much effort, Prometheus kept his eyes peeled forward, keenly surveying whatever was to come.

From the end of the hallway Prometheus could have sworn he heard a deep and guttural growl, accompanied with a small spark. Eventually, Everhart turned his attention on the vermin, but the rats did not seem to notice. The one nearest the door finished his enchantment and the thorns retreated. "Marmot, let's go. Go, go!" one of the rats at the front squeaked.

But something had caught the first rat's attention. He sniffed the air in bewilderment until his nose twitched, catching a specific scent. His beady little eyes darted straight to Prometheus, staring at him as if trying to figure out some strange puzzle. Prometheus smiled. The rat's head cocked sideways.

"Marmot!" squeaked the third rat. He looked back. "*Marmot!*" he screamed.

A singular lapse in concentration was all it took. Through the mist, a barrel of turquoise fire curdled its way to the end of the hall, sending the vermin guards up in a blaze of matching fury. Everhart screamed and covered his face, jumping headlong against the farthest wall of the cage. Prometheus's eyes stung as the heat smashed against his retina, yet he did not look away. The heat and ash of the fire licked his face, but it did not enter the cell. He sat and watched as it burned its way through the fur and bones of his would be guards. Prometheus wondered to himself if he had ever seen something so beautiful.

Eventually, the smoke settled and a single eyed, dark pelted wolf stepped through the embers of the burning hallway. His paws tiptoed lightly past the two freshly singed skeletons. The wolf's lone eye was the only part of his body that seemed to be on fire.

With a wistful smile and welcoming arm motion, Prometheus had finally found his reason to speak. "Well, well, if it isn't the mighty wolf!" he said with a laugh. He waived his arms in the air in a mock greeting, blood trickling to the ground with every sway. "Setting things on fire in a tree, eh? That would not exactly be my first plan of attack."

The wolf stepped forward, lowering his head menacingly. "I don't have time for your tongue, human," he growled as he surveyed the area. "Silence it or have it burned out of your slimy mouth."

Prometheus nodded. No sense in wasting a perfectly good tongue.

"Good," the wolf said, taking in the caked blood covering Prometheus. "What happened to you?"

Prometheus shrugged. "Multiple failed attempts to escape."

"Humans," the wolf snarled, though Prometheus could have sworn it was meant as a smile. The wolf looked back nervously. "We don't have much time. If I got you to the boy and the cat, could you use that book they stole?"

"Of course I can!" Prometheus lied happily. "You get me to the boy and the cat, and I can make sure that no rat or owl or snail or panther or whatever damned ghastly animal that ails you will ever be your boss again. We could make your wildest little wolf dreams a reality." Prometheus smiled to himself, turning on his most grandpa-esque charm. It was almost too easy.

The wolf looked around, hesitant. "If you betray me, I'll rip your throat out." His single eye was trained on Prometheus like an arrow, taut and ready.

"That's only fair," Prometheus nodded.

Again the wolf checked his surroundings before heading out. He signaled for Prometheus to follow. Prometheus uncrossed his legs and stood, cracking his back and brushing himself off leisurely.

Mr. Everhart crawled to the front of the cage. "What about me? Don't leave without me!" He stood, trying to get through the door. With a singular fist, Prometheus sent Mr. Everhart's bloody jaw and all that was attached to it back into the cage. Everhart landed with a thud.

"You're staying here with your furry little friends," Prometheus said, cracking his knuckles. "I couldn't bear the thought of being the one to separate you from them."

As the wolf led the way down the still burning hall, Everhart curled into a ball, alone with a cracked jaw and the distinct smell of burnt rats. "Enjoy your berries, Adrian." Prometheus walked down the hallway without a single glance or second thought back.

After four nights of no fires and nothing to eat but the leaves crunching underfoot, accompanied of course by a delectable drizzle of stream water to wash it down, Prometheus found himself wondering if his dear friend Mr. Adrian Everhart had gotten the last laugh. At least Adrian had those silly magical berries in his stomach.

Having a wolf for company did not really help silence the sour squeezing of a belly that needed filling. It also did not make much of an open invitation for great conversation. Prometheus had never realized how much he actually enjoyed the subtle art of syllables until he was met with plain growls and "Keep moving" to satisfy his literary palette. Ever since they left the gigantic redwood that harbored those pesky paranormal animals, subtly nicknamed the "Animal Kingdom" by Prometheus, he had thought of one thing and one thing only. He never should have left his one true love behind.

"Where is it, human?" the wolf asked again. The wolf was a skittish animal, not seeming to trust anyone. He did not even trust a sweet old man like Prometheus.

"It's up ahead, through the next clearing," Prometheus said soothingly. He was finally starting to recognize the surrounding woods as his hovel and ground, though it was inexplicable to him how oddly close the Animal Kingdom stood. On the entire trek to his woods, he made a mental note of each location to make sure he could find his way back. Regardless, no matter what happened from here on out, he was in a good mood today.

But when Prometheus walked into the clearing where his house should have been, no amount of screaming or kicking at the desolate ground would reveal to him the secrets of the cat's magic. The man cursed loudly and proudly, crawling in circles on the ground as he beat himself up over having lost his house. He assured his new wolf friend that this was the exact place where his house was, or at least where his house should have been, but Quinn just sat on his haunches, chuckling deep within his throat. How excitable humans could be. Quinn rather enjoyed watching the cocky man shout nothings at the ever insolate, yet inanimate woods. The wolf just could not bring himself to tell this human professor of the slight trail of honeydew and thistle that hung in the air, a scent most commonly coupled with the magic of a certain feline.

"Are you angry, man?" Quinn asked, a wicked grin splitting his muzzle. "Have you seemed to misplace something?"

"My house is gone! It vanished!" Prometheus said, trying to calm himself but to no avail.

Quinn looked around innocently. "Are you sure this is where it was?"

"I think so," Prometheus said, studying the woods from his knees. His face was wrangled in an ungainly fashion, attempting to think. "Yes. Yes, this is it! Wait . . . . No?" He beat the ground with his fists as if trying to fight for a lost memory. "Damn it, I cannot seem to remember."

"What was so important to you?" asked Quinn in earnest. His tail flicked against the ground. "You have your fur, I will provide the meat, and though your paws may be inadequate, they're still highly useful things."

"My gun," the man named Prometheus said with a snarl that would make most wolves proud. "My gun was in my house."

"Ah, yes, your teeth," Quinn said, nodding knowingly to himself. "I forget that man is nothing without his metal. Regardless, we should keep moving if we want to catch them any time soon." Quinn stretched his hind legs, making a mental note of the wondrous moment that had just passed, and started off deeper into the woods. Prometheus stood reluctantly and began to follow. He stole more than a few looks back, checking the tree line and surrounding brush, knowing more and more that this was exactly where his house had stood the further he left the exact spot. It was as if the knowing of its existence was hidden to him. He shuddered and began to understand.

"It was that damned cat, wasn't it?" he grumbled.

"Most likely," the wolf answered back. Prometheus could almost feel the smirk the wolf was carrying, if wolves could indeed smirk.

"How do you even know where the boy and cat are going?" Prometheus said, desperately needing to change the subject. He did not like knowing he was outplayed, much less by things out of his control, but he had been wondering exactly where they were going themselves.

Quinn grunted. "I know because I've been there before. They have the book, correct?"

"Apparently," Prometheus nodded. "So?"

Quinn shrugged, keeping his pace. "So, they're going to the dragon's lair."

Prometheus stopped, bewildered. "The dragon's lair? Why on earth would they return there?"

Quinn turned around, his head tilting in honest confusion. "Because, that's where the book takes you. I thought you said you could use it?"

"Of course I can use it!" Prometheus lied. He had the book for a good time, but he had honestly never gotten it to reveal any secrets. In truth, he had hoped the book would unlock the secret to the one thing in this world he did not understand.

Magic.

"I just don't get why the cat's book would take them to the dragon's lair is all," Prometheus said, recovering. He always patted himself on the back for his mental dexterity in tough situations.

"The cat's book?" The wolf's eye was barely a slit, its eyebrow slightly raised. "You think that the Book of Illumination was written by the cat?"

Prometheus nodded slowly, not quite understanding the problem, but Quinn just shook his head in rebuttal. "No human, it was not. It was written long ago by the dragons themselves."

Quinn turned then, walking ever forward. Prometheus scolded himself for being so stupid. Again, he found himself being surprised by the cat. He quickened his pace to fall in time next to the wolf.

"Why did the dragons write it then?" Prometheus asked. It was an honest question.

"I do not know, I wasn't around." The wolf shrugged. "All we've ever been told is that it is imperative to the cycle. One dragon, one egg, one book, the cycle must continue."

"What the hell does that mean?" Another honest question, though this time not as politely poised.

Quinn fell silent in response, his head dropping slightly in shame.

"You don't know?" Prometheus laughed.

"Again, no." Quinn cleared his throat, his nose twitching. "This was all before my own birth and knowledge. It's a saying that's been passed down through the ages, yet as my brethren grow weary, the knowledge seems to fade quicker and quicker. I'm not sure anyone truly understands outside of maybe Abraham and the older members of the council."

Prometheus peered into the woods, his gaze falling on nothing in particular. "Knowing that they knew something I did not would tear me up inside. I'm not sure how you lived with it for so long."

Quinn shrugged. "I had never questioned it."

Prometheus could not help but feel sympathy for the silly magical animals as a whole. If there was one thing he actually cared about, it was knowledge. There was nothing worse than feeling in the dark.

Quinn stopped, sniffing the ground, feeling the earth through its myriad of smells. He stretched out his paws and pointed with his snout. "This way," he grumbled, turning slightly to the left.

"How do you know the way to the dragon? Have you been there before?"

"Of course I have," Quinn said, keeping to the path. "I was the council's messenger to him, though it's been forever. He mainly likes to keep to himself."

"I've noticed." Prometheus remembered the dragon perfectly. He also remembered never being so terrified in his life. He hated that any one thing could have such an indescribable grip on his emotions. He spat again. Yet another instance he was not in control.

"How do you know where you're going?" Prometheus said, keeping in step.

"From here, it's a simple path," Quinn said nonchalantly. "I could really walk it in my sleep." The wolf pointed to the sun with his snout. "Straight west, follow the tree line, until you come upon an enormous cave that happens to have a dragon in it. You really can't miss it."

"If it's so simple," started Prometheus, "how come no human knows its existence?" It was an honest question.

"As I understand it, and it's not exactly my area of expertise," Quinn said, stopping. "No human will ever find it because it's hidden from the realm of human . . . perception? Yes, I think that is the word."

"Then how come I was able to come across it with the cat?"

Quinn shrugged. "I would assume that the cat gave you the knowledge, or shielded you from not knowing at least.

"So I can still see it now?"

"Most likely," Quinn said. "It's something your body doesn't forget, unless the dragon wants you to." Quinn chuckled to himself. "Though, if the dragon knew of you at all, I'm sure you would have been long dead."

Prometheus face twisted in sarcasm, though it quickly turned into a shiver. The thought of the cat casting any sort of spell on him was putrid. What other sort of trickery could the feline have played?

"I feel the same way," the wolf nodded with a grunt, catching the shiver. "The cat's knowledge is a remnant of the old days, an area he seems to have a deep awareness of. I, sadly, have none." Quinn touched his snout to the earth again as the ground in front of him began to part. "You see, I understand the earth and the wind in the same way." As the wolf looked upward, a swift current of wind began to swell around him, raising thickets of leaves hovering over the ground. The earth opened up in perfect circles under his paws, before shooting upwards and twirling around the wind in a controlled manner.

Prometheus could feel the shivers down his spine and he knew it was not from the sudden gusts of wind. He stepped back, utterly disgusted. "*Magic*," he said. His lips curled in disgust.

That night, after a day's worth of unsubtle hints of weariness in the forms of sighs and grunts, Quinn decided to make camp. He picked a small little clearing, with just enough tree coverage overhead so as to keep out prying eyes, but not enough that he could not sense anything lurking in the trees themselves. Just in case, Quinn lowered his snout to the ground and breathed in heavily. He could almost taste the different minerals in the ever-shifting bouquet of rocks and dirt and sand deep within the ground. The wolf exhaled, letting himself breathe out the earth itself. In response, an enormous cloud of dust erupted into the air in a dome like appearance. For a moment, the dust seemed to hang there in a place outside of gravity and law, before it trickled back down to within the earth's crust.

Quinn was not surprised to find the man named Prometheus studying his every move. The man seemed perplexed, his eyes darting around frantically as if he were intent on finding the secrets of what just occurred. Quinn grunted at the absurdity. Like a human could find the secrets of anything.

"What did you just do?" Prometheus asked with no attempt to mask his disdain.

Quinn tried to formulate the word, to find the meaning of the feeling, but only a deep and throaty rumble escaped from within the chest. He stopped and sniffed, perplexed. "Your language does not have an adequate word," he said. It had been a long, long time and many human languages ago since he had tried to explain the feelings of nature itself.

"I know over thirty languages," Prometheus said. "Try me."

"No human language will ever be enough," Quinn chuckled as he scratched his snout against the ground. "What I just did was . . . protection? To protect us from being detected by others, to mask our scents and sounds."

"Like a ward?" Prometheus asked. It was if Quinn could see the cogs turning and processing inside his human skull.

"Yes, like a ward," said Quinn hesitantly. The wolf did not understand this word exactly, but he did not feel like letting Prometheus in on it.

Prometheus sat forward, the moon catching a glint in his eye. "More *magic.*"

Quinn scoffed. "You say this word, but you know nothing. *Magic* is for humans." The word left such a vile taste in the wolf's mouth. "*Magic* is like your guns or planes. It's harsh and undeveloped. It's barely a rude understanding of the earth and the sky and the wind and how they taste and how every scent travels within them. There is no word that could begin to describe the feeling of what is around you and the intricacies of how to interact with it. *Magic* is tricks. It's fake and false. This is not *magic*. This is knowing."

Prometheus shrugged. "Well, someone *magically* made fire appear to toast a couple helpless little rats straight to the bone," he said with a wicked grin. "I just figured that was you." He set his head on the ground, staring at the sky.

Quinn lowered his snout, his eye darkening. "I did what was necessary. One would imagine that humans would be more considerate of those who rescue their hides."

Prometheus propped his head up on a shoulder, feigning innocence. "Oh, so that fire was you?" He sighed. "I wonder how you started it if not for magic, being as how I don't remember any wolf having the finger dexterity to light a match."

"It was not *magic*, boy," Quinn said, growing tired of this game.

"Then what is it?"

"It is knowing!" said Quinn, his single eye lighting up at the thought. "I understand the essence of the atmosphere and the substance of each mineral in the ground. I know each scent, taste and sound that flows through each of them, and with that knowing comes manipulation. Those of us wolves who still remember learned long ago how to spark it."

"Show me," Prometheus said, a little too intently, though Quinn could not see the harm in it. No human could ever speak the language of the soil and heavens.

Quinn held his lower jaw out, his bottom teeth pressed against the top. His snout twitched as he watched the air, feeling its every twist and sway. He felt the tug of three different currents, enough for a small flame, and instinctively pulled them into a concentrated point in front of his muzzle. As the air rapidly turned to a deep shade of yellow, he snapped his teeth together so quick a spark ignited in front of him. A fireball shot forward towards Prometheus, evaporating into smoke just before it reached him.

Prometheus did not so much as twitch. He just sat with his same wicked grin, nodding his approval as he wiped the gathering soot from his brow. "I don't know what you did to the air to compress and twist it so quickly, but the use of the fangs as an ignition for initial combustion is a nice touch." The man's eyes darkened gleefully. "Honestly, it's not a bad trick, though it certainly seems like magic to me, regardless of your *knowing*."

Quinn rolled his eye and placed his head down with a sigh. The wolf was too old to fight it. Magic was such an ignorant word.

"Tell me," Prometheus said as if his mind were playing with a puzzle, "is that how the cat produces flame? I've seen it once or twice, yet I don't remember a spark."

Quinn growled at the mention of the feline. "No, the cat does not understand the way I do." His mind raced with the images of that daring blue flame enveloping his pack. His stomach began to churn. "I'm not exactly sure how he knows or where his knowledge comes from; it's different for each species. In the same way, he could never understand the feeling of the earth like a wolf can."

"I see," Prometheus nodded. "What about trees?"

Quinn's head tilted in curiosity. He sat up. "I don't understand."

"Well, like the rats you burned, some of the rodents in your Animal Kingdom seemed to have a *knowledge* of the plants and foliage, like of the cage that held me." Prometheus shrugged. "Is this common?"

"No," the wolf began slowly. It was an innocent enough question, but Prometheus had only shown himself to be anything but innocent. Quinn mulled over his words carefully. "I have no knowledge of trees, it is true. The cell itself is grown by the squirrels and rats and other vermin and comes from a very different awareness."

"Like the cat's ability to change perception?" Prometheus asked.

"Yes," Quinn nodded. "Exactly like that."

As Prometheus rolled over, Quinn hesitated before letting himself find any rest. The questions seemed common enough, though anything from Prometheus's mouth that was not alarming was alarming within itself. Still, he could not see the danger in it per se, as no human had any understanding to begin with. He begrudgingly let himself drift off into a dreamless sleep for which he was thankful.

When Quinn woke, it was not the sharp pain of the ever thickening and twisting thorns tightening around his every inch, nor the immediate sense of immobility that crushed his pride; it was the wicked man hunched over him, congratulating himself with a twisted grin at his own cleverness. The wolf tried to move, squirming back and forth, but each movement was met with a sharp pain in every inch of his body. He knew he was trapped.

"How?" Quinn managed to grunt through the thorns. Prometheus held up the scraps of his shirt sleeves and opened them for Quinn to see. It was then he knew why his movement was met with a sickening twist of thorn and vine, keeping him pinned to the ground, completely immobile. How Prometheus had ripped any part of the squirrel's cage away, much less sustained it through their travels, was a mystery to him. "*What about trees?*" The question rang clearly through his brain. Quinn snarled, cursing himself again for being so dimwitted.

Prometheus's lips cracked into a smile reminiscent of the ever-twisting thorns. He let the rest of the thorns and vines drop onto the ground from the depths of his torn and tattered shirt. The batch was no bigger than Quinn's paw, really, but as Prometheus held his hand out, the thorns grew toward it. Prometheus grabbed onto it, his hands bleeding anew. His eyes gushed with delight.

"The little wolfy, so easy to catch in his sleep!" Prometheus laughed to himself, dancing in the pale moonlight with a wave of his hands and knocking of his knees. *What about trees, Mr. Wolf?* the old curious man says! *Can wolves play in the trees, Mr. Wolf?*" Prometheus laughed and jumped through the air, landing next to Quinn with a thud. Quinn met him with a snarl.

"*No, you silly human!* the smart wolf replies!" cackled Prometheus with a gnarled and twisting finger. "*We have no knowledge of the trees!*"

Prometheus stood and stretched, cracking his knuckles and surveying the area. "You know, the best part wasn't outsmarting you. I figured I could do that easily enough. It wasn't even watching as you were encircled by your newfound home of thorns. Hell, it's not even knowing that you know I would not have escaped from that prison without you in the first place!" Prometheus bit his bottom lip, his eyes beginning to tear in delight. "No, my new favorite friend, the best part is knowing that you were stupid enough to trust me." Prometheus leaned in, his voice dropping to a whisper. "Who is ever stupid enough to trust me?"

Prometheus stood and with one last look at the stars, he checked his bearings and headed off deep into the woods. "Who knows?" he shouted back, his voice crackling in delight. "Maybe I can even learn to love magic!"

CHAPTER EIGHT

It did not take an intricate knowledge of the human psyche to tell that Derek was not ready for what lay ahead. The closer the book took Derek to the dragon, the more the cat could feel Derek's resolve crumbling. The boy's face was growing increasingly pale and the palms and pits on his body were reeking more and more from the gathering sweat and the lack of bathing. He seemed skinnier, more gaunt in the face and cheek bones, though it was not from a lack of nourishment. In fact, the cat had fed Derek handsomely throughout the nights and days they spent together.

The cat would hunt, though it was barely enough of a chase to call it that, and subsequently trap the lesser animals who had now given up the old ways. He would then help Derek in the preparing of the meal and make sure Derek had his fill. Sure, the first night Derek had watched the cat make his way into their campground he was a bit skeptical at the bird the feline carried in his teeth, but the boy's belly soon got the better of him. It was the preceding nights that began to worry the cat: the nights where the cat would attempt to start a conversation, something the cat was not apt to do, but only find himself greeted to a growing set of grunts, offhanded looks and other signs of growing discontent. Even as the cat was sure Derek had eaten his fill, still Derek was finding ways to shed weight.

The cat had assumed Derek was not made so fickle and fragile like the rest of his kind, but then again he was facing probable and most imminent death. Such a thing seemed to affect most men.

The cat watched Derek stare absent-mindedly into the floating blue flame that offered a light on their surroundings. He constantly twiddled Prometheus's gun in his hands and chewed on his inner lip as he mindlessly picked at a crack in the gun's framework. Over the past few nights, Derek seemed to have a growing fascination with the cold piece of metal. At first he started cleaning it. Mindless polishing, really, but over the waning hours of the night Derek could be seen digging the dirt out of each little crevice the revolver had. The cat tried again and again to strike up conversation but in the end, he would end up staring and waiting patiently in the ensuing silence. In truth, it was the only thing he knew to do.

But tonight was different. After another long day of the cathartic crunching of leaves and twigs under his clumsy feet, Derek did not hesitate to sit down and pull the gun out. When the cat had called a cease to their movement, leaving the treetops to pull Derek out of the spell of the book, the boy was already lying on the ground, his head resting on his backpack and the gun held firmly in his hand.

It was the first time the cat had seen Derek hold the gun as if he actually meant to use it.

"You know, I've never even shot a gun before," Derek said emphatically. He held the gun out in front of him and pointed it into the sky, seeming to aim it at some heavenly foe. "For that matter," he continued, "I don't think I've ever even held one before this." The cat's tail twitched patiently. Just because a human begins to talk does not always mean he is looking for a conversation.

"Derek the dragon slayer," Derek said with a heavy tongue, lowering the gun. He peered off into the night, his eyes flitting in a random fashion. He stared as if he were weighing the pros and cons of each word that crossed his mind.

And so the cat struck first. "Derek, can I ask you a question?" he said, calm and decisively. The innocent question seemed to make Derek hesitate at first, but he gathered himself quickly.

"If I said no, you'd ask it anyways," Derek replied, a tad cold.

"Very true," the cat said, smiling at the quip. He was almost proud.

"Then yes," Derek sighed. "You can ask me a question."

"Good," the cat nodded. "As long as I have your permission."

For the first time in what seemed like forever, Derek truly made eye contact with the cat. He did not budge more than his head, but the smile that followed put the growing tension at ease.

"I seem like a smart creature, do I not?" started the cat.

Derek shrugged.

"Well, do I seem like the kind of creature that would risk the entire fate of the world on someone I did not think was up to the task?"

Derek had no answer, verbally or visibly. He let the question hang in the air as he stared at the cat, the wheels inside his human brain convulsing around the notion. The cat could tell the boy did not believe it possible himself, but he could find no rebuttal. His eyes twitched as the thought sank in. He sighed and turned back to the stars overhead.

"No," Derek said quietly. He chewed his lip and rested the gun on his chest. "No you do not."

"Precisely," the cat said, surveying Derek peacefully. "In the end, a dragon is a beast like any other. Yes, it is larger and quite a deal more menacing than most of the other beasts you're likely to encounter, but it is still mortal. It can still be killed, or murdered, or slain as you put it."

Derek did not respond.

"And, you must admit," the cat pressed on, "if there is one thing humans know how to do well, it is killing things. Your kind has thrived off of it so much that they have created a perfect instrument for the task."

Derek looked at the gun resting on his chest.

"Yes, Derek," the cat said as if knowing what Derek was thinking. "It is just metal, but it certainly does its job."

"What if I miss?" Derek asked quietly.

"You won't miss. I'll be guiding you."

"Oh, yeah?" Derek sat up, unconvinced. "What if I do miss? What if I miss and it devours me or burns me into the ground? Can dragons actually spew fire? How big is it anyway?"

"All very pertinent questions," the cat chuckled. "Again, you won't miss, you can't be devoured by the dead, and yes it would burn you into the ground if I weren't there. And now that you mention it, the dragon is actually quite large from what I remember, but I wouldn't worry about that because it just means a bigger target."

Silence ensued. The cat's tail began to ease its swaying as the cat felt Derek's own heart beat begin comply.

"Satisfied?" the cat asked.

Derek laughed to himself. "No."

The cat shrugged. "But you're still here, are you not?"

Derek had no answer. The boy only stared straight into the cat's eyes, weighing the small feline with each breath. The cat could not find a single trace of what the boy was thinking and it worried him greatly.

"Would you lie to me?" Derek asked.

"Yes." The cat said.

"At least you're honest about it." With that, Derek nodded, turned over and actually found some real sleep.

When Derek awoke, he somehow knew it would be hard going from there on out. He let his eyes adjust to the stark sunlight. The way ahead was uphill mostly, through thickets of thorns and brush, stemming from an endless array of sand colored trees that reached longingly to the sky. It did not affect him as much as it once would have. He stood, inhaled and brushed off the bits of earth still sticking to him. Even as he stretched his legs by walking around the outer rim of the campground, there seemed to be some added pep to Derek's step. He began to notice how his feet fell lighter, more agile and with a greater care. If he did not know any better, the leaves and twigs underfoot seemed to crunch less.

The cat was gone by now, keeping mainly to the treetops as it always did, jumping from branch to branch overhead. It had said it was scouting, keeping an eye to the sky and its nose to the winds. Derek understood the sentiment of wanting to be ready. He was glad for it and thought nothing of it.

With a final stretch and a yawn, Derek adjusted his backpack and placed the book out in front of him on the ground. Then, he drew the gun and its bullets, placing them next to the book, counting nine bullets in total. His heart began to race, but he steadied his hand and began to load the chamber as he had practiced. He stopped and stared at the loaded weapon. It was his shot at saving the entire world. With everything he had witnessed the cat do, he was truly beginning to feel they really had chance. How big could a dragon be, anyways? If it lived, it could die. He laughed to himself then as the notion caught in his brain. *Derek Agons, the dragon slayer.* It was better than being Derek Agons, the high school dropout.

Derek eased the handle of the gun into his open and ready palm, squeezing the metal gently. He had gotten used to the weight of the weapon now as he tucked it into his pants. He knelt forward, taking a deep breath before opening the book. Instantly, the surrounding area seemed to dim as the book breathed in the light and lifted itself off of the ground. At this point, he was getting used to the prickling sensation of the magic as the book warmed up. Whatever it was in the particles floating around him, in the bouncing reflections and brightness, especially the brightness right before a foreboding shadow, every bit of it seemed to fuel the book.

He blinked. In an instant, the fireflies appeared. One by one, they created a path deep into the woods to his appointed destination. They crawled out from under tree branches and shrubbery, from under rocks and leaves until they eventually settled down into a perfect walkway. Each was a different size and glowing a little more or a little less than the next. It was like traversing through a million glowing snowflakes, with no two looking alike. Even in the brightest of sunlight, their abdomens glowed so brightly it seemed like the very air around them was dimmer. Derek stood, gathering the book up in his other arm, and waited for his favorite part.

From behind a tree some odd yards away stepped out the girl that Derek longed to reach. She caught Derek's gaze and smiled knowingly. Derek's heart leapt at the sight. It was the same smile every time, and every time he felt his cheeks flush. She broke the look and turned toward the fireflies, catching one in her hand. Derek watched as it flew around her, flittering about. Whoever she was, wherever she came from, she was the single most beautiful thing Derek had ever seen.

And so Derek, as he had done for what seemed like an eternity now, walked through the endless forest toward the girl, through ever-changing trees lines, boulders and thickets of thorns. With each step and each day, his purpose became clear. He was meant to follow the book's simplest of instructions: just one more step. It was never a desperate one more step, which he realized after the sun had fallen halfway through the sky. He giggled warmly. Just being in this moment was a fulfillment of his purpose on earth.

From overhead, the cat kept his distance, creating an aura of wind and illusion so as to shield his presence. He hissed when the book began to glow, the hairs on his back prickling. Below him and quite a ways away, Derek's face was glued to the old manuscript, his head down and his mouth mumbling. The astonishing thing was the way Derek never once looked up, but he always seemed to navigate the forest in perfect harmony with its every twist, tree and root. He never stumbled, never fell. Each step was perfectly placed with the right amount of weight distributed to it.

The cat was well versed in manipulating the emotions of weaker beings, but this was beyond him. The book always seemed to lead wherever it wanted. It was an off-putting sight at first, but only because it was yet another thing the cat did not understand. The list of such things was slowly growing and the cat did not like it one bit.

It had taken a week or so of trailing Prometheus from a distance before the one time explorer had finally let himself open the book. Even with the cat's immense distaste for the old man, he knew Prometheus was exceptionally cunning. It would only be a matter of time until he started on the path to understanding the mysterious book the cat had heard so much about.

After a day or so of no movement within Prometheus's lair, he had burst into the wood clearing, wielding the book and two magnifying glasses. He set the book on the ground, opened it and then placed the magnifying glasses between it and the sun, sending it into a glowing frenzy. The cat was alarmed at first, obviously having seen the human trick to set things ablaze before, but he knew better than to question the human explorer. Even in the animal kingdom, Prometheus's exploits were unrivaled where humans were concerned. It was said he had traveled deep within the seas, scaled the inside of mountain passages long forgotten, and penetrated forests deeper and thicker than any human before him.

It was also said he never traveled alone. There was a team of experts for each expedition he set forth on. Yet he always came back alone. His novels and discoveries about the human world and where it met with the animal kingdom were the reason the cat learned to actually read English in the first place.

Prometheus had stood over the book that day with a maniacal look etched across his face. He thrust his hands into the air to catch the perfect angle through the magnifying glasses. As the sun shone through each one, the book never actually caught flame. Instead, it seemed to gorge on the very essence of the light itself. It was the power of the sun, the scent of the heat, the heart of the flame that the book longed for. The pages never smoked, never even crackled. The book's only response was to glow.

It took another week for Prometheus to realize the book would not grant him any wishes. After failed fires and mounds of used matches, the book would just absorb the flames, only to lead Prometheus in circles around the woods. He would walk the woods, sometimes for days on end, but eventually he would return home in frustration. Late into the night he could be heard ranting and raving about how he would make the book do his own bidding, that he would not go back. It did not take long for the cat to know the book was attempting to lead Prometheus back to the dragon's lair. The cat smirked at the thought. It was not often that things worked out exactly as one wanted.

The day the cat approached Prometheus with a business proposition, the cat was not surprised at his nonchalance with coming face to face with a talking animal. The man only shrugged and said he had seen weirder. What did surprise the cat, though, was that when he began to fill Prometheus's head with stories of dragons and a magical book that could grant his every wish, he had signed on to the task without a moment's hesitation. His eagerness should have alarmed the cat to some degree, but the cat's own curiosity had gotten the better of him. It had been a long time since there was something the cat did not know of. He had lived for so long and discovered so many curious things that all it took was a book hidden by the council for the cat to break their most sacred of rules: humans must not know they exist. A silly rule in truth, and one the cat had never much cared for. The cat knew the second the council found out he had broken it he would be fugitive number one, but he did not care. It really had been such a long time since he had something to be curious about.

But even then, the cat never would have expected that being inside the dragon's cave that fateful day would ruin any hope he had of settling the churning in his stomach. It was not fair, really. The book itself was not hidden; in fact, it was in plain sight. All it took was a simple little path, tucked away in the back of a dragon's lair and the cat was hooked. Now, every time the book was used the cat kept his distance, always starting up his own protection measures to make sure that whatever was leading Derek did not know of the cat's presence.

So when Derek cleared that final tree line and stumbled into the perfect little clearing at the foot of the mountain, the cat patiently waited his turn. It was almost bittersweet, for he had come to appreciate the boy's untimely company. Still, he knew what must be done, and so he thanked Derek Agons for his inevitable sacrifice. It would not be forgotten. It was with his help that the cat would finally know what secrets the dragon thought he could hide from the waking world. A cruel and misguided thought in the end. No one hid anything from the cat. He breathed in the surrounding air, churning it into a senseless aura where nothing existed to a knowing eye or snout and crouched in wait for the perfect opportunity to finally slink back inside.

Curiosity was a cruel mistress indeed.

CHAPTER NINE

When Derek broke the tree line, it felt like the entire atmosphere around him had changed. The air was thicker here, more concise and specific, the breeze more faint. Even the way the sun came down from above seemed just a tad bit dimmer. He hugged the book to his chest, thanking it with his human embrace. He was finally here, finally arrived at exactly where he was meant to be. The fireflies were gone now, their soft linear light no longer leading him. He had nodded in admiration as the last one seemed to blink out of existence.

He looked for the girl, but she was nowhere to be found. The thought did not surprise him. In fact, he somehow knew that she would not be here directly. Not yet anyway. He sat on the ground, placing the book neatly in front of him and checked his surroundings patiently. The sand colored tree line almost held a perfect half circle around the rather large clearing at the base of the mountain he had reached.

A single large opening stood at the base of the mountain. For a moment, Derek wondered what sort of large creature the cave could hold. He shrugged. It was a fleeting thought and it was not all that important.

In front of him, the book was now pulsating furiously with the light it carried. That was odd. He had never seen it so worked up. He nodded, breathed deeply and contentedly placed the revolver on the grass. There would be no danger here. This was paradise.

He blinked. The cave opening seemed to shift as if the deep shadows within had crawled their way forth and disappeared. He scoffed. Shadows could not crawl. He looked at the book again and immediately his eyes began to tear up. The light now escaping from within was blinding. Derek shielded his eyes but instantly regretted it for such an action was not supposed to be his nature. The book was his comfort and his everything. Why would its warm light be too immense to be seen? A warm gust of wind hit his face. Odd. He did not remember the wind carrying the smell of char and meat.

When he uncovered his eyes and let them adjust, the illusion broke. He was not sitting peacefully and he was not sitting alone. No, in fact, he was standing and staring straight into the eyes of a dragon. Twenty feet long with white scales that glittered in the sun like a flame igniting, the dragon stared back. His head hovered barely a foot away. Spittle dribbled from his mouth as his breath hit Derek in the face like a steam engine. Every muscle in Derek's body tensed.

If Derek had not known better, he could have sworn the dragon was smiling.

Immediately, Derek jerked around, finding the book lying open on the ground behind him and Prometheus's revolver lying uselessly beside it. He jumped and grabbed the gun, rolling and pointing it straight at the dragon. Or, at least, he would have been pointing it at the dragon, if the dragon had not disappeared completely. His heart caught in his throat, his pulse pounded away in his ear. He shook his head, trying to clear his vision. Was it always this hard to breathe? He twirled around, pointing the gun frantically this way and that, but the clearing was completely empty. The dragon had vanished into thin air.

It was then he heard the chuckle, a deep and guttural sound that grinded through the air. The sound reverberated in Derek's chest. Did his heart just stop? Derek turned and turned, checking every possible angle, but the dragon was nowhere. He clutched the gun in both hands and tried to calm his shaking.

Another warm gust of wind caught on his neck as the smell of char and deep ashes tickled his nostrils. Derek flung himself forward, twisting around with the gun held out. The dragon stood over him and this time Derek knew for certain the beast was smiling. Before he could get a shot off, the dragon chuckled again and dissolved, his blazing white scales taking in every little detail of the colors in the surrounding area as they shimmered out of existence.

Derek stopped his body from shaking long enough to regain his stance, but failed to steady his breathing. His palms slipped on the grip of the revolver from sweat. He fumbled around the hammer of the gun for too long. The metal was slick and unresponsive. He tried to catch his breath, slowing it down long enough for the oxygen to actually reach his brain for thought. His thumb caught the hammer and finally cocked it back. The click was music to his ears. He crouched over and kept the gun in front of him.

Where the hell was the cat?

"You're going to hurt someone if you're not careful, boy," the dragon's voice boomed through the clearing. "Those things are meant to kill."

"Show yourself, beast!" Derek squeaked. It was not the most intimidating of commands, and he definitely could have done without the break in his voice, but Derek was indeed facing a dragon that could magically disappear. What was worse, the dragon was toying with him. Derek shivered. As terrible as Derek was at estimations, the ancient lizard had looked at least thirty feet long and as wide as a small building, every inch of his cool white scales bristling with muscle underneath. When Derek had opened his mouth, he was happy anything came out at all.

"Humans," the dragon said, chuckling again. "So quick to command and yet so fragile."

Derek's ears twitched at a rustling over his shoulder. He spun on his heel, firing three shots wildly in the direction of the sound just before a massive and glittering white tail caught him in the chest. The ground spun underneath him, his arms flailing wildly as he was sent through the air. With a thud and a crack, he landed directly on his left ankle and felt the bone snap cleanly under his weight. He looked down, though he knew he should not have. The sight of the protruding bone was more than he could bear. He screamed, clutching at his ankle in agony, but the sound was completely enveloped by the roar that was now escaping from the dragon. The beast roared again, the sound absolutely thunderous. It filled Derek's entire being, sending his vision fading and making his heart pound harder and harder. If the heavens did not split under the roar, Derek's head sure did. He looked up, blinking heavily, and forced his eyes to adjust to their surroundings.

In front of him, barely ten feet away, the dragon sat on his back clutching at his tail. He rolled back and forth on the ground as he wailed, his hind legs kicking about. A trickle of deep and thick blood flowed from a nick in the dragon's armor. He roared again, but this time with less than half the fury. If Derek had not known any better, he would have thought the dragon was almost whining.

"Are you both quite finished?" A new voice cut through the dragon's roaring. Derek whipped around. From within the tree line where he had emerged himself, a beautiful and majestic female now walked lightly towards them. The deep white linen dress she wore shone brightly in the sun. Her light auburn curls bounced gently against her shoulders with every step. Derek knew her in an instant.

"He shot me, Tella!" the dragon roared again, his voice cracking in distress. He stared down at the blood oozing from within his tail. "I can't believe it! He actually shot me!"

"Oh be quiet, Caelus," the girl in the white dress said. *Tella.* For some reason Derek felt as if he had known the name before it was said. Pain shot through his leg and yet he did not care. His head was spinning again. He could not stop himself from wanting to know everything about her.

"Of course he shot you. You attacked him!" Tella continued. She approached the dragon with an air of ease, kneeling gently beside the great beast. The dragon held out his tail, and the girl named Tella inspected it. "It's barely a scratch. Don't be such a baby."

"I was just playing with the boy!" Caelus scoffed. He pulled his tail to his mouth and began to lick the wound like an oversized dog. "I didn't mean anything by it."

"Yes, and we both know where your playing has gotten you before, Caelus," she said as she patted the dragon on the head. She turned and started walking toward Derek. "Humans are fickle and frightful creatures these days, not like in the past. One cannot just assume they will not shoot first and ask questions later."

The dragon thumped loudly in response, sitting up on his haunches. A brief puff of smoke escaped his nostrils as he crossed his arms across his chest. Derek stared in disbelief. This was the great and terrible beast intent on destroying the world? The dragon caught his gaze and promptly stuck out his tongue in response.

Derek felt the panic creep in as Tella closed the ground between them. He searched frantically for the revolver finding it on the edge of the clearing, completely out of grasp. He cursed himself for letting go of it, but then again he had been flung through the air, so it was a trivial thing to be worried about. He gritted his teeth and tried to stand, but the weight on his cracked ankle sent him reeling to the ground. The searing agony ran like lightning waves through his entire leg, but still he pulled himself up and twisted around, ready to face his fate.

To his surprise the girl named Tella was sitting next to him. She crossed her legs and caught his gaze in an amused and perplexing stare. Her eyes seemed to glisten from within, perpetually smiling regardless of the rest of her face. Derek's heart jumped. With her being so close, it was easy to see the freckles that peppered her cheeks, the way her lips seemed eerily smooth. There was not a moment's worth of age in her; her face was without wrinkle or fault. In fact, it seemed smooth, almost luminous. What was more, he found it hard to place the color of her skin. This girl named Tella was clearly fair in complexion, yet it was not the color of a normal girl he would see at school. Her skin was more akin to the lightest shade of escaping light from within a newly lit light bulb.

Tella seemed to glow.

Derek looked over his shoulder to where he left the book, but it was nowhere to be found. Only the dragon remained there, still sulking and licking his wounds.

"Looking for this?" Tella said. Derek turned. The book floated out from behind her, filled now with an almost peaceful luminance. All at once it surrounded Tella with a slight halo of light. Her glow was absolutely overwhelming. It filled Derek with confidence and understanding, putting his mind at ease. The pain of his ankle was all but forgotten.

"I don't understand," Derek forced out. He bit down on his inner cheek, flinching at the pain. It felt so natural to be in this exact moment, but he would not be caught in the illusion again.

Tella beamed in response. Such a soft and sweet thing it was. If it was going to be her only reaction to anything, Derek was glad it was so overwhelmingly pleasant.

"Of course you do not understand!" the dragon boomed with laughter, the sound as deafening as his roar. His white scales glistened and clattered as his body shook in mirth. With a final huff and a flex of his wings, the dragon rolled onto his forelegs and started making his way to them. The ground shook under every step.

"You are but a human child," Caelus said, sitting himself down next to Tella. "You're not much more than a whelp in the scheme of life with a broken understanding of how the world began." He picked at the now coagulated wound on his tail. "You do not even know your own past, much less the knowledge of ages. How could you understand anything beyond your metal and cold electricity?"

"Shush, Caelus," Tella said, soft but stern. The dragon rolled his eyes, letting out a contemptuous puff of smoke from his nostrils.

"No, that's not it," Derek said, beginning to gain his own composure. "You're not evil?" He pointed to the dragon. "You're not trying to destroy the world?"

"Destroy the world!" Caelus roared with laughter, flame shooting out in bursts from deep within his throat. "Destroy the world he says!"

Tella shook her head sympathetically. "We are not evil and we are most certainly not trying to destroy the world. We're the ones trying to save it."

"Save it? Save it from what?" Derek shifted his weight uncomfortably. His brain was so overloaded, he was surprised he could even form that much of a sentence.

"Can we show him, Tella?" the dragon said unable to hide his amusement.

Tella hesitated. "I don't think that's such a good idea."

"Please? Don't make me grovel." The dragon said with a smile. "Groveling is not very befitting of a dragon."

"Show me what?" Derek could not fight the curiosity that now swirled inside his head.

The dragon sat forward, bringing his enormous head level with Derek's. Derek could feel the heat that seemed to radiate from the dragon's very being. Caelus's teeth flashed in a blinding grin. "Would you like to see how your world began?"

The words hung in the air. Derek looked at the girl. Tella was virtually unreadable as she stared at him, gauging him with every thought. He caught his breath, looked back to Caelus, and nodded slowly.

"It's not a very happy story," Tella said quietly, a deep sadness filling her eyes in recollection.

Derek shrugged with a smirk. "I don't really like happy stories, anyways."

Caelus roared in answer, slapping his tail on the ground in absolute delight. Tella only sighed. "Fine then," she said, nodding slowly. "Don't say I didn't warn you." She looked to Caelus. In response, the book lifted into the air, floating directly above the dragon's head. The dragon gave Derek one last rueful smile before he sucked in deeply, huffed twice, and enveloped the book in a furious stream of molten lava from deep within his chest.

The world exploded then in a flurry of twisting colors, streaming together in every direction possible. The light itself was blinding, but Derek could not look away. His eyes began to tear up as a million different shades, shapes and objects danced through his blurring vision.

CHAPTER TEN

From deep within the cave, the faint and flickering sound of gunshots trickled their way down to the cat's ears. He chuckled to himself. Of course, there was always the possibility that Derek was made of stronger stuff than the cat had originally assumed, and he did enjoy the brief taste of delicious irony at the thought of the almighty dragon being taken down by a mere boy, but it was a fleeting thought. The gunshots were followed quickly by an almost intelligible set of roars that most certainly told of Derek Agon's untimely death.

The cat could not tell exactly how long he had been traveling down the dark and twisting cavern, but he was not so sure he cared. Moments like these were what he longed for, what he continued to live for. The cat had snuck past the dragon and Derek in what would be a very short-lived bout, thinking to himself that he would never forget the sensations that filled him as he crawled back into the dragon's lair. Quickly, for the cat knew he did not have much time, he had hopped his way across the mountains of treasures and trinkets that filled the lair. His nose had picked up the scent he was looking for almost immediately. Tucked away in the back of the lair stood the tiny little cave, pulsing with the most sinister knowledge the cat had ever tasted. The cat's body had begun vibrating then, his tail swishing back and forth with excitement. How long had he schemed to get back to this place? It felt like another lifetime completely. The cat sneered to himself. That's because it was another lifetime, two to be exact. For everything to actually fall into place meant it had to be destiny.

The cat walked along, losing himself in the dark and twisting shadows of the cavern trail. He marched deeper and deeper into the earth until even his own senses could not catch their bearings. The trail had been packed with trivial defenses thus far: vines and rocks levitating like trip wires, scents and sounds that would attempt to speed out to the animal that placed them. The cat only scoffed in contempt. He had been setting these sorts of brutish traps for lifetimes now. His tail wagged happily as his nose caught another barrier, this time set from a keen understanding of wind and its interaction with mist. Without a thought and with a flick of his tail, the barrier loosened and dispersed into the darkness.

Whenever the cat's final life eventually passed, he knew he would remember this moment for eternity and into whatever lay beyond.

A new scent caught the cat's nose, yanking him from his thoughts. He stopped and inhaled, caressing each smell out of the surrounding cavern. The very taste of it churned the cat's stomach, making him feel uneasy. This was a new taste, a new scent, a new flavor of decaying earth and crumbling roots. It was unlike any the cat had ever witnessed. It meant he was getting close.

And he was, for after what felt like an odd mixture of both hours and sometimes barely minutes, the cat came upon the end of the trail. It was a small and unassuming little piece of cave, pitch black to every sense. The darkness itself was so thick that the cat's eyes could not even adjust to it. He filled his lungs and released slowly, letting forth a small burst of his patented blue flame into the air, before encircling it with just the right amount of wind pressure to keep the ball afloat. The cat let his eyes adjust to the blue light bouncing its way across the now lit room.

In the middle of the room sat a small black jar. The cat sniffed the air before approaching it carefully. Even from afar, he could tell that the vase was absolutely ancient, though not by any means of seeing. Its outward appearance was eerily perfect; rounded at the bottom with a quaint lid neatly placed over the top and not a scratch nor a speck of dust on it. It almost seemed as if the jar rejected any form of decay from within. Though, as the cat drew nearer, he knew it was not the jar's outward appearance that made it seem ancient. It was the hellish magic that reverberated from deep within its porcelain veins.

The cat licked his lips, his brow furrowed. A thing more curious than this could not possibly exist. The cat was certain he had discovered and tasted every possibility the once exciting and now predominantly dull and human world had to offer; yet, after all of his lives and all of his deaths, countless centuries and innumerable discoveries, he had never seen the jar's like. The cat allowed himself a slight grin from exhilaration and focused all his energy on the object before him. Slowly, the cat's claws extended as they dug their way into the ground. He moved his paws in unison, gathering the very pulse of the earth they touched. It had been a while since the cat had attempted to learn a new sensation, a new taste, a new feeling. He wondered if he was still half as good at it as he used to be.

Breathing just deep enough to steady his heartbeat, the cat felt his tail began to sway. He knew what he was looking for. Whatever lay inside the jar had a pulse, a piece of knowledge rooted in some unknown quantity. For the cat, this knowledge was like music, a pounding and reverberating feeling from deep within. Each sense contained a tune, a beat, some hint of a note to be heard. The cat's tail stopped moving completely, standing directly upright in the air. He stared at the jar, allowing his eyes to lose their focus and slowly he caught the pulse. Beat by beat, his heart caught on to the sound of whatever lay hidden in the jar. It was faint, barely discernable, but nothing was too far off for the cat to understand. Back and forth his tail swayed faster and faster, picking up speed. A taste caught on in his tongue, a whisper caught in his ear. He did not know how to feel about it specifically but somehow he felt he had tasted it before. Curiosity began to set in, but the cat did not let the feeling shake him. He centered his focus on a second taste, one different from the barriers and traps that were placed on the trail down here. The earlier traps had felt like they were formed in a more direct fashion, as if mimicking a human metal lock. A strange thought. The cat had never known any animal to attempt to represent a human invention. The cat's tail wagged and wagged until his heartbeat match the swaying. The cat had found the tune. He let go of the breath in his chest and watched the murky cave surroundings evaporate into a normal atmosphere. The cat's golden eyes flickered in his small blue flame, still standing tall ahead. He knew he stood alone with his prize.

As quickly as the barrier had vanished, the lid of the jar began to shake. The cat watched the vibrating increase until the lid seemed to shimmy its way onto the ground. His heart pounded from excitement. That cat blinked. No, that was wrong. His heart was not pounding at all. Was it even beating? He tried to shake his head, to clear his thoughts, but found himself unable to control a muscle.

Slowly, from deep within the tiny vase, a single dark cloud of dust rose into the air. The tiny dust cloud stopped directly in front of the cat, seeming to pulse from within. The cat watched as it grew and shrank in perfect time with the pulsing. Instantly, every hair on the cat's body stood on end. This was not right. The cloud was cold and dark, a thick and ever-changing visage of impenetrable mist. In fact, it seemed to be made of thousands of particles, thick with the most ominous knowledge the cat had ever sensed. The cat tried to breathe in, tried to gather the air out of the surroundings enough for fire but could not. Every inch of his being was overwhelmed with a multitude of sensations: fear, desire, resentment, fault, necessity. The cat tried to blink, but could not. He tried to think, but could not. His tongue grew heavy as he could not decide whether to laugh, to cry, to shout or scream in anger or pain. He wanted to drop his head to his chest, to hang limp, to do anything, but every muscle in his body was overwhelmed with each new sensation.

And then the little cloud of shadow exhaled.

Instantly, the room filled with darkness. Had the cat closed his eyes? He tried to blink, but it was useless. The poor lost feline did not know where his body began and ended. All around him, the world exploded into a white and blinding vision of stars and earth. He had no sense of time, no equilibrium to hold on to. Both horrors and miracles flashed across his mind, though he had no taste for either. Everything was happening at once so there was no need to think a specific thought. Instead, all thoughts existed in their own space and matter. Most he did not understand, though some stuck to his mind like a forgotten word. Bright white beings journeying through a myriad of elements, filling atoms with their light until they withered one by one into a field of blackened trees. Dust and darkness encapsulating a bottomless land, and at its center, a monstrous castle and the tower that held it in a perfectly white sky. Then, the earth sat in silence with its three parted lands. No sound permeated the thought, only a single knowledge of the malice that strummed along in unison until it shattered into a swirling dimness. Finally, the seas burst forth and sunshine reigned down upon a still and waiting earth.

The cat saw all in its enormity and somehow it did not frighten him.

Slowly, ever so slowly, the vision faded, as if someone knew the cat was thinking it. When the room returned to normal, the cloud floated directly in front of the cat's face. He watched in utter horror, his mind flooded and ready to burst. It was a feeling he was not quite accustomed to, and certainly one he never wanted to experience again. The cloud moved forward, keeping its dense and misty innards afloat. The cat wanted to twitch, but could not. Instead, his ears perked up at the faintest sound of a hum. From deep within the cloud, a slight whirring began to fill the air as if the cloud was trying to control its breath. Again the cat tried to move, to twitch, to do anything, but it was hopeless. All the cat could do was allow a singular emotion to flood every inch of his being: fear.

"I NEED A VESSEL."

The sound ripped through the cat, coming from deep within the recesses of the cat's brain. It was not a voice, not a particular timbre or fidelity pulled from a specific vocal cord, it was more of a thought.

"YOU ARE NOT MY VESSEL."

The voice reverberated again, this time louder and with more fervor. The cat felt his body shiver under the weight. These were the last thoughts the cat ever wanted to have.

"THE CYCLE MUST CONTINUE."

And with that, the cloud shot forth and escaped the secret little cave that had been filled with so much curiosity. Over time, the cat did eventually regain feeling, though he wished all at once he had not. As the cat's own conscious thought began to settle back inside his skull, he could only scream, hiss and collapse to the ground, his body shaking uncontrollably from deep within his bones.

For the first time in his existence, the cat was completely and utterly ashamed.

CHAPTER ELEVEN

Derek shook his head, forcing his eyes to adjust to his surroundings. He knew that he should have been surprised to find himself standing over the earth, but instead he found himself completely calm. He flexed his broken ankle, testing it gingerly by bouncing up and down. It was, of course, completely healed. Derek thought nothing of it. He had seen way too many movies not to know exactly how the dream sequence part worked.

He crouched down, holding his hands at his side in concentration. "Fire! Go fire!" he yelled as he punched both hands over his head in unison. No fire exploded from deep within his aura, but still he was not to be hindered. He paused, calmed himself and cleared his mind before flexing his wrists and fingers in tandem. "Lightning!" he screamed, his arms slicing through the air with a thunderous fury. "Wind burst!" he yelled and flailed his arms around his body in wild circles. Still nothing. After talking animals, lava spewing dragons and magical floating book girls, he figured his own shot at magic was worth a try.

He looked below to the spherical mesh of green and blue spinning peacefully beneath him. He knew it was earth, for he had seen it from afar plenty of times in his science classes, but something seemed off. His eyes focused through the cloud coverage as he surveyed the continental layout of the planet. Each continent below was now amassed perfectly together in the middle of the world instead of scattered across the oceans. It was like every piece of land fit perfectly together in some gigantic puzzle. Only the northern and southern poles remained as he once knew them, though their glacial mass was substantially smaller than he remembered. The earth turned underneath him and he tilted his head in confusion. Odd. The ice surrounding both the north and south poles were perfectly aligned, down to every minute detail. They spanned the exact same width and height, despite of how the rest of the earth was just one gigantic continent. Still, it was a minor detail. Derek looked to the new conjoined mass of land floating peacefully alone and knew that it was good.

"Welcome to the beginning of ages."

Derek turned and found Tella leaning against Caelus, the book floating peacefully overhead. They made an odd trio at first glance, but now Derek found it hard to picture them without each other.

From its floating perch, the book spewed forth an infinite rainbow of colors. Each new color fell gently to the world below, disintegrating as it fell out of view. He tried to follow the trails of color into the distance but failed. He could feel each strand of color twisting into a finite shape as it spun and weaved its way into the mirage around them, but the colors themselves stayed firmly latched in his peripheral vision. He could never quite catch their full meaning.

"This is the earth, right?" Derek said, motioning to the lands before him. "Why is it so . . . connected?"

"This is how it came to be, Derek," the dragon said. The giant beast began to shift uncomfortably, the wheels turning in his head. He looked as if he was reliving a memory both immense and dreadful. Caelus cleared his throat. "The world you inherited is but a fraction of its former and once great beauty. That which you know now is broken."

Derek stared down, raising an eyebrow at the strange thought. Below, he could see thousands of tiny patches of thunderstorms beginning to break over the center of the massive singular continent. They spread in a flashing dance across mountain ranges covered in snow and boulders so big Derek could still make out their faint outlines. Just then, a corner of the great continent erupted in red and brown and smoke, as if a hundred volcanoes had broken their seals in unison. Red streams flowed across the land in a flurry, enveloping miles of greenery and foliage, until each red blot soaked into surrounding desert.

"Who broke it?" he asked, watching the earth dance below him.

"I did," Tella replied softly.

"You?" Derek turned and stared in disbelief. "How is that possible?"

Sadness flashed across Tella's eyes. At her silence, Derek looked to Caelus, though it was clear he shared her pain. "Let us show you," the great beast said quietly.

The dragon's head swiveled towards the book. Derek shielded his eyes, unable to watch the flames consume it. He allowed himself a glance at the brilliant light but quickly closed his eyes as they stung and filled with tears. Instead, he relaxed and let the changing environment surround him like a warm and enveloping breath, catching deep within in his chest and toes. It sent his skin tingling and his hair on end. The very essence of where he stood in time was shivering into something new and magnificent.

Derek opened his eyes. He now stood atop a mountain, overlooking an enormous valley. He tried to guess the valley's length, but it was mind boggling. It did not seem to end. All he could tell was that it was wider than it was long and filled with an endless supply of monstrously tall trees. He scanned the valley from right to left and blinked, unsure if his eyes were playing with him. From where he stood, the trees appeared a dark shade of green, but every time he turned his head, they shifted to a bright maroon in his peripheral. Everywhere he looked, the valley seemed to be completely covered in the countless thickets of treetops.

That was, of course, until he noticed what lay in the exact middle of the valley. Dark and reminiscent of a nightmare, the valley's center was nothing more than a void like hole in the ground. It looked like it had been carved out and replaced with absolute nothing. Not absolutely nothing but *absolute* nothing. Derek squinted, unable to see what exactly the clearing held. His eyes would not focus on the spot. He coughed and a small inkling of bile crept into the back of his throat.

His thoughts were interrupted by the sound of laughter, speech and general business. He turned around and almost fell flat as he stared into the mountain he stood on. Its insides were hollowed out, leaving room for a city hidden within. Flickering lights caught in a cascade against an endless sea of houses. Each house was made of a different material. Vine thatched canopies, complete with intertwining bamboo shoots, glowed in a hardened maple like substance. Boulders were molded into domes, caked with mud and frost and mineral. Ice fortresses stood fifty feet tall, their crystallized walls catching every flicker of light as they overwhelmed the smaller houses in their frozen wake. Even the stalactites were mounted against each other in unique patterns. The combinations were endless.

Derek heard a squeak behind him. He turned around yet again. This time, he found a small boy sitting on the ledge of the mountain. Small and with a thick rustle of black hair, the boy sat and kicked its feet in the air as he overlooked the valley.

The boy giggled and turned his head to the small fox resting on his shoulder. The fox was also pitch black, his fur seemingly richer than the darkest crevice of the mountain behind them. The fox's ears perked up as the boy pointed forward, his finger stretching out over the valley below. Together, they nodded and turned. Derek stared in amazement when he caught the fox's eyes. No pupils, no definition, just pure silver. The fox and the boy blinked in unison.

The boy's eyes were the exact same as the fox's.

Suddenly, the sun was fading over the valley and the boy was sprinting into the mountain. He jumped down, landing on a spiral path of stone stairs and disappeared into the flickering darkness.

"Follow me," Tella said, now standing at Derek's shoulder. She took his hand and led him into the mountain without question. Down they marched until they came upon a house made of large white roses, each crystallized in place to form a monumental, forty-foot domicile.

Inside, the crystal castle glimmered with walls that caught every bounce of light. In the middle of the room, Caelus stirred and twisted around to Derek and Tella walking in. "You're taking this well," the dragon said. "I remember my first time learning the ages as a young hatchling. It can be quite overwhelming."

"You're not from this time?" Derek asked.

"Of course not," the dragon scoffed. "Do I look this old to you?"

"Well, you're a dragon, so I just kind of assumed." Derek shrugged and bent down, feeling cool crystal floor in his fingertips.

"I am barely a couple millenniums," the dragon huffed. Small patches of flame exploded from his nostrils. "You humans have no sense of true time. I'm still a baby to my ancestors."

"Wow, really?" Derek said, unable to hide the sly smile creeping onto his cheeks. He stood and met the dragon face to face. "You're a baby?"

"Yes, that is what I said," the dragon replied slowly. He twisted his head in question. "What of it?"

"Well, nothing really," Derek began with a shrug. "It's just if you're a baby, and well, to my race, I'm practically an adult, so relatively speaking—"

"Don't even dare go there, boy," the dragon said quickly.

"—No, but seriously," Derek continued. His eyes twinkled in the shimmering crystal light. "Relatively speaking, I'm older than you."

Caelus stared Derek down with a snarl, but the boy stood his ground. They stretched out their necks in tandem, each glaring and snarling. Caelus's lips quivered and broke into a smile. The great dragon broke into laughter, the front of his nostrils exploding in tufts of smoke and fire with each giggle.

"Older than me. He actually said it! *Older than me!*" the dragon managed through his mirth. The dragon smacked Derek on the back with his tail, sending the poor boy smashing to the ground on his hands and knees. "I think I like you, boy! You've got more backbone than the rest of your kind." Derek stood, shaking his head gingerly. He could not help but chuckle along with Caelus.

"Quiet," Tella said, silencing the unlikely pair. She did not turn when she said it, she only clasped her hands behind her back and let the words do the talking.

"She's always like this when it's time to get serious," the dragon attempted to whisper in Derek's ear. "Stick with me, I'm more fun." Tella turned, a single eyebrow raised. Derek could not hide his smile. Dragons were absolutely dreadful at whispering. He could tell he was going to like this lumbering beast named Caelus a lot.

In the middle of the crystal palace, the fox and the boy now stood in concentration. The boy lifted his hands in a triangle shape overhead and the fox's eyes began to glow a piercing silver light. The ceiling overhead exploded in a bright and self-sustained turquoise flame.

Derek eyes widened. "Did they just do that together?" He had seen the cat perform a similar trick multiple times but never so big or so brilliant, and the cat had never done it with a human.

Tella nodded warmly. In front of them, the fox and the boy sat down patiently, their fire raging overhead. "No one knows for sure who began the bonding," she said, her eyes burning with fervor, "but it was discovered that the inherent understanding of the animal could be magnified through a bond with a human."

She turned to Derek, making sure he was paying attention. "Now you must understand, Derek, not every beast formed such a bond. In fact, many never felt the need. In some of the older circles, it was even considered a very deep and treacherous blasphemy. But, once connected, the bond could allow the human and the animal to do unimaginable and wondrous things."

"Like break the world," Caelus said, his once playful tone now vanished.

"Like break the world," Tella finished quietly.

A roar ripped through the air. Above them, the crystal ceiling swirled inwards, shaking the building with its intensifying movements until the roof groaned and sprouted open like a blooming flower. A single pair of wings flapped their way through the opening, before expanding in a blinding array of color, speed and ferocity. The wings were long, easily more than twice the size of Caelus's, though it was the dragon attached to them that truly was a sight to behold. When the dragon settled, Derek could tell the ancient beast was actually smaller than Caelus overall, despite the enormous wingspan. Looking at this newer dragon's face, though, Derek knew exactly what Caelus meant when he said he was just a baby of their species.

Piles and piles of crackling and endless scales enveloped the smaller dragon's face and chin, forming an almost beard like concoction that drooped off of his chin.

Each scale was a different shade of brown, some so dark they looked black, others so light they seemed to be made of an ever-deteriorating piece of sand. Long, leathery ears hung down below the dragon's head, ever swaying as he bobbed back and forth in thought.

It was the eyes that really told the dragon's age. Derek could see that Caelus's eyes were surrounded by single, large scales in freshly packed rows; none were cracked or even remotely bothered by the test of time. This newer dragon had eyes that were surrounded by a million different scales, each shattered in every direction, with newer scales forming deep within the cracks. No two scales were alike in shape, size or color. No two scales broke the same way.

The smaller dragon folded his wings and lowered his long and muscular neck. It was then that Derek finally noticed the girl that had been riding gently on the dragon's back.

"Tella," he exclaimed. "It's you!"

"Yes, Derek," Tella said, watching the other version of herself step off of the brown dragon's back. "It's me."

Derek could not help but compare the two versions of Tella before him, though it was for naught since they were identical in every way. They both shared the same shoulder length auburn curls, the same flowing white linen dress. The only difference was the shimmering crown of crystal roses that surrounded the other Tella's head. She wore it effortlessly and gracefully, though Derek did not expect anything different. Everything the girl did was elegant.

"Alexander," the other Tella said with a nod. She walked across the crystal floor, her flowing white dress shimmering in the walls. "Where are Hagan and Barret?"

"Still asleep, I assume," squeaked the little the fox, his bushy tail wagging in delight. The boy nodded with a smile.

"Aden," Tella said, smiling at the fox. "I did not ask you."

"Yes you did," the boy replied. The fox and boy giggled to each other.

The great brown dragon chuckled, his twisting beard and drooping ears jiggling in tandem. "Just let them have their fun, Tella," he said. Derek's heart melted. The dragon's voice was the purest and deepest baritone that had ever rumbled through his chest.

"Yeah, Tella," a new voice boomed from above, engulfing the room with its mirth. "You need to loosen up!"

High above, toward the highest point of the wall, the crystal's began to crack and shatter in a web like pattern. Piece by piece, they churned inwardly, twisting at a single point until they exploded in unison. The wall shivered in response, filling with mist until it dissolved to reveal a sparkling new doorway. Beneath it, the mist hissed and gathered until one by one, the droplets stopped altogether, forming a dazzling set of crystal stairs.

A gush of icy wind blasted through the doorway. The boy and his fox shivered in their skins, their flame almost flickering out overhead. The great brown dragon shook his head. "Always an entrance."

The other Tella only rolled her eyes.

From within the newly formed door stepped an eight foot tall polar bear. Its fur was a perfect sheen of white; almost every single inch and clump of it was blinding to the eye. The bear yawned, brandishing rows of sharp fangs piled within its maw, the two largest hanging loosely against its lips.

On the polar bear's back rode a dark skinned man, yawning in unison. "I heard that, Gansu!" he laughed. The coupling of the bear and the man was wholly absurd, yet it was easy to see their bond was absolute. Every trait they each carried was equally shared. Both were broad of shoulder and proud of face, complete with finely tuned beards that flowed down below their chests. When the man caressed his beard, his polar bear friend stood on his hind legs and attempted to follow suit. The man screamed like a little girl then, squirming to hold on to the bear's back in a flurry of arms and legs. Derek could not tell if they were insane or just naturally defiant to nature. Of course, the fact that neither of them wore a shirt and both of them wore pants certainly did not help.

"So good of you to join us, Hagan," the old dragon growled, watching the polar bear and man make their way down the stairs.

"Of course, Gansu," the dark skinned man said, smiling ruefully to the dragon. "You know I wouldn't miss this for the world." Hagan winked at Alexander and Aden. "*Literally.*" The polar bear winked his agreement.

The energy in the room was palpable. Even the other Tella could not contain her excitement. This was a group that had survived centuries, a group that had clearly been through hardships Derek could only imagine. It was the type of group he had always wanted to be a part of.

"Then let us begin!" Gansu slapped the ground with his tail in thunderous agreement.

The room exploded in flurry of motion, each pair of human and beast exiting the cave in a flash of their own unique knowledge. The other Tella hopped onto Gansu's back, his massive wingspan already in motion as they shot into the air. She held out her hand and a small group of tornados began to form around Gansu's body. Quickly, she quickly closed her fists and each one exploded in a gush of wind, propelling them through the ceiling.

The fox jumped onto the boy's head, wiggling his tail and adjusting his weight. The earth underneath began to rumble. The boy squatted, stretching out his arms so as to steady himself. He shifted his feet. The fox's silver eyes absorbed the light around them. With a crashing of the earth below, both Alexander and Aden exploded in a burst of fire as they shot through the open ceiling like a missile. They disappeared behind a trailing line of thin silver smoke.

The polar bear and the dark skinned man stood still in their places, unmoved and stoic. Again, they yawned in unison. Hagan ruffled the fur on the polar bear's large head before closing his eyes. Together, they inhaled, holding their chests puffed out in place. Derek blinked. Nothing happened. Derek waited and waited, but they just stood still and silent. When Derek blinked next though, they were gone. Only a thin veil of mist remained in their place.

"I want that," Derek said with a laugh. "I want to do all of that."

"You?" Caelus asked. "You are nothing, boy. You could never understand what it is to feel the mists!"

Tella watched as Derek and Caelus continued to squabble, losing herself in her own thoughts. How long had it been since she had relived this past? How long had it been since she actually *lived* this past? She could not say. Countless millenniums had gone before her eyes now, and each one melted into the next, forming one long and silent memory of keeping the world together. It had all been so simple before; nothing more than a group of friends exploring the great continent that was once the earth. She remembered the first time she and Gansu witnessed the majesty that was the polar bear and his rider in the old acres' arena; miles of golden stock that stood like towers reaching to the heavens. In the arena, the man and his polar bear were an absolute force to be reckoned with. Countless bouts of wit and strength they faced against the world. For all of their years at the arena's center, no two creatures ever bested them in a match of intelligence or force. What was more, in the knowledge of mists and silence, they were the most gifted pair she had ever seen bond.

Though, of course, that was before they had reached the great southern coast. They had spent a week traversing its beauties. Great white sand reached for miles, peppered by the sparse lonely mountains in the distance. Tall, black boulders ran along the shore in droves. In front, the water was a deep violet, offset by the ever-raging skies overhead. It was an odd contrast, though it was said that if you stood and stared into the violet sea before you, you could gain a year of life equal to how long you held your breath. A silly notion. Still, it did not stop the four of them from trying.

It was then that Gansu had picked up the scent of bile, blood and rotting skin. In a patch of the beach's signature black boulders, they found a small boy coddling a dead baby fox in his hands. Both were completely alone, completely naked and almost half dead. Both were soaked in blood and ash and scarring flesh. The boy was barely breathing.

When they attempted to bury the fox, the boy came to almost instantly with a gasp. They tried to console him, to tell him it was too late, but the boy only screamed in angst. It was Tella who noticed first. She turned around to bury the fox, to continue with what had to be done, but stopped in her tracks. In front of her, the little fox sat perfectly still and perfectly alive. He smiled at her nonchalantly, before bounding happily to rest in the boy's lap. Tella would never forget the dark glimmer in the fox's stark silver eyes.

She allowed herself a small outward frown at the thought. She never could get Alexander to speak of exactly what had happened, even after years of travel and trust. Once or twice she had probed his emotions, but to no avail. Aden always kept both of their minds completely locked away with nothing more than a smirk. Tella had never pushed the matter, exactly. She just assumed the pair of them would open up and talk about it when the time was right.

The sound of Derek's laughter and Caelus's increasing self-righteousness broke her from her thoughts. She was glad the dragon was taking to the boy. It had been a very long life of solitude for her young dragon friend. Tella knew how much Caelus longed for some sort of connection outside of the little she could offer herself. Every time a dragon passed on, the egg would hatch, bringing forth a brand new dragon and egg in its wake, ready to understand its role. Each time, Tella would retell the story of the breaking, pretending that it got easier. Such a fleeting lie, she knew. The story broke her heart more every time she relived it.

Caelus caught her eye, shaking her from her thoughts. She knew the look well, telling her it was time to carry on. She nodded to the dragon and Caelus nodded back before he engulfed the book in another bale of flame.

Derek stared into the dragon's fire for as long as he possibly could before his eyes welled up in tears. The colors danced through his eyelids and the world settled around them. Every sense Derek had tingled whilst reality gained its composure. Little by little, he knew his body was growing accustomed to the sensation. The colors poured forth from the book and the light itself was blinding to be sure, but Derek almost reveled in the feeling. His stomach shifted with the last bit of the settling world. He was even getting used to fighting back the urge to vomit.

When Derek opened his eyes, he recognized the location almost immediately. Before him stood the hollowed mountain they had just come from, silhouetted against the sea of trees that now separated them. He turned and let the world around him sink in. Directly in front of him, at the edge of his toes, stood a hole in the ground at least a mile wide. He could not explain it, but he knew that the hole was not made by any conventional means. It had not been dug or hollowed out. The hole's insides just did not exist. It was completely void of any mass or particles. Derek felt his brain pulsing, trying to work through exactly what it meant. Every inch of the opening was dark and endless. He did not know much about magic or knowledge but he could feel just by looking at the expansive nothingness that it was filled to the brim with power. His eyes began to glaze over. He did not want to stare anymore, in fact he did not want to have sight at all. This *void* was such an endless and menacing provoker of the unknown. He felt himself drop to his knees. Slowly, he leaned over the edge and tried to peer into its deepest recess. His eyes could never possibly touch the bottom, but he could not help himself. The thought was overwhelming.

"What is it?" he asked quietly.

"A hole in the ground," said Caelus. The dragon chuckled at his own cleverness.

One by one, Tella's group began to appear around the hole. The polar bear and the dark skinned man emerged first, stepping through a thin veil of mist while they shimmered into existence. They released their breath in tandem, offering a smile and a nod to each other. From above, the dragon Gansu fell in a flurry of wind, wings and fire. He landed softly, his gigantic wings pillowed by a group of controlled tornados held by the other Tella. She hopped off the dragon's back and steadied herself, fluffing her dress. The fox and the boy were last, though they were not far behind. They landed in a front flip, the little black fox clinging to the boy's back. Alexander stood and the fox hopped onto his shoulder as they rejoined their friends.

"It is a void, Derek," Tella said, stepping up beside him. She looked out onto her friends, her face glowing with pride. Caelus joined them solemnly, the book following closely behind. Derek could feel the shift in their group's energy. Even the book seemed slightly dimmer in comparison.

"To us, though, it was the last great mystery of our time," Tella continued, her face locked in determination. "This hole in the ground was the one place no living thing, be it spirit, animal or human, could get near."

"Why?" Derek asked. He watched the boy Alexander pick up a rock and toss it out over the void. The rock went up in smoke, dissipating into nothingness as it came into contact with the expansive black hole. Alexander giggled excitedly to Aden. The other Tella scolded him, but it was not heartfelt. Their entire group was brimming with excitement.

"Energy is a fickle thing." Tella peered into his eyes, blocking his vision. "Energy is just that, it is energy. It is neither inherently good nor is it inherently bad, at least, not so far away from the source. It is to be molded, it is to be mended, and it is to be formed by those who can understand it." Tella signaled to Caelus. The dragon nodded and breathed in deeply before letting forth a small burst of fire from his nostrils. The fire folded within itself, splitting into a mixture of steam, air and embers. The elements danced in a circle. The dragon huffed slightly and a single ember landed gently on the edge of Derek's nose.

Tella flicked the ember with a fingertip, letting it float into the air. "It is the source itself that changes its understanding."

Derek grabbed his chest, rubbing his hand gently over his heart. "So this pressure," he said with a slight grimace. "Is it the energy?"

"It is as much as I am willing to show you," Tella nodded. "The actual pressure was much, much more intense."

Derek followed Tella's gaze out across the void and forced himself to breathe. He could feel the pressure growing steadily. His blood began to pulse in his veins. "What was the energy?"

"We did not know. No one could explain it, but many of the animals and humans of the day felt it was better not to try. They were happy and their lives were more than comfortable. Why chance what this power could possibly be?" Tella shook her head. "But it was not enough for us. The power from the *hole*, as Caelus so eloquently put it, was so absolutely immense that the group of us could not help but be drawn to it. Though, just based on the sheer volume of the energy, it was easy to see why the world before us had decided to seal it off. But as time went on, we grew complacent and thus we grew curious."

Derek turned his head, only to find that he and Tella now stood in the air, directly in the middle of the void. Tella took his hand and nodded for him to look down. His hand clenched. There, down below him, was a deepness he had never witnessed. It was not necessarily evil, but on the other hand it was not necessarily good. What it was, was completely unknown and overwhelming.

He gasped and shook his head. "Did you forget to breathe, Derek?" Tella asked knowingly. He nodded in astonishment, forcing his eyes to focus. When that did not work, he shook his head violently to regain his bearings.

"You have to understand that our decision was brought on by an age of unrest," Tella said, her voice a simple whisper. "It started off with just a simple *What if?* in our small group of friends, but as we began to voice our opinion we were surprised to see how many others were thinking the exact same thing." She turned her gaze out across the void, awaiting something. "What surprised us more was the overwhelming response we got from our inquiries."

Suddenly, the leaves began to shake and rattle in the treetops overhead. From deep within the forest, adjacent to where the other Tella stood with her friends, a family of nine-foot grizzly bears lumbered from within. Each was covered in a dark maroon fur with splotches of a deep and patterned gray. On each of the bear's shoulders rode a small human. Each person's eyes were slanted and sunken deep within his or her face, though their pupils shone brighter than any Derek had ever seen. Even then, as bright as their eyes could burn, nothing could outshine the sheen of their bright red hair.

From above, a thick black cloud of smoke puffed down from the sky like its own contained locomotive engine until it landed lightly on the void's edge. The cloud dispersed, leaving an old and hunched woman sitting in its place. On her shoulders sat two small brown owls, hooting and bobbing their heads simultaneously. She smiled toothlessly to them, sending them into a frantic squawking before they began ramming their heads into each other in excitement.

The treetops began to shake and bend violently toward the ground. With a furious twang, a family of oversized apes shot themselves into the air in a series of back flips and howls before they landed gracefully on the ground without a sound. Together they hollered, pounding their fists into the dirt and grass underneath. Atop each rode a sleek and slender woman. They too hollered in jubilation, jumping off their partners' backs and joining in the commotion.

On yet another side of the void, the trees parted for a massive turtle, fifty feet in height and built like a mountain. The lumbering giant strode slowly forth from within the great forest. Every inch of its shell seemed to be made of straight boulder, piled endlessly upon itself. An indiscriminant man crouched atop the beasts head, hunched over and decrepit. The man scratched his poor excuse for a beard and overlooked the void with satisfaction.

"The question still stood, though," said Tella, breaking Derek out of his thoughts. "What if we were to dig deeper? What would we find? Would we unleash something great and terrible upon the earth? What if what was lost down there, whatever was the source of that tumultuous energy, what if it was terrible and locked away for a reason?" She stared at Derek, her eyebrow raised slightly. Derek knew she was hoping he would know the answer.

He smiled softly, knowing indeed that he did. "Or," he began, quietly meeting her intense gaze, "what if you were to dig deeper and find something wonderful that no one else ever knew?"

"Exactly," Tella said, motioning to the void. Every inch of the hole's edge was now surrounded by a pair of animal and human, standing together in triumph. "Something is not evil just because it is unknown."

Derek blinked and found himself back at his original spot along the void's edge. Caelus shifted nervously next to him. He prodded Tella gently with his snout. "It's time to watch now," he said, nodding toward the void. Tella pursed her lips in determination, facing the memory head on. Any hint of hesitation had melted away. Every line of her body was now arched perfectly, though not a single muscle seemed tense. Each part of her visage beamed in determination.

Caelus pulled himself onto his hind legs, squaring his shoulders. The dragon stood tall next to his partner, facing the memory in tandem. The dragon's jaw tightened, his teeth grinding together. "You too, Derek," Caelus said, using his tail to turn Derek's head forward. The four of them, since Derek counted the book as its own entity now, stood and waited as one. Every creature in the surrounding forest waited with them.

Every bonded animal and human around the hole closed their eyes and linked hands in concentration. Derek wondered if he should do the same. Slowly, the earth began to shake, increasing in intensity as the wind began to howl. Derek could feel the pressure growing and pulling at his chest. He looked up. The trees began to groan and gasp. Each towering oak began to bend inward toward the hole, the treetops themselves being pulled forward. The surrounding air shrieked and crackled then, sending shivers down Derek's spine. Above him, the clouds darkened to a thick and rippling black. They pulsed from within, growing in size. The low rumbling of a distant thunder growled past his ears. As if set off by some singular gunshot, one of the clouds burst into a mass of lightning, shooting forth thick tendrils of blazing electricity in all directions. Each cloud the lightning touched followed in its wake until the entire sky lit up as one.

It did not take long for the surrounding area to turn into complete chaos. Between the wind and the earth's increased trembling, some of the smaller humans and animals began to lose their footing though their concentration never broke. Even as the trees around them began to snap in half and the earth underneath became completely unbearable, still they kept their eyes shut. Still they kept their minds honed in on whatever personal mantra they were so keen on. Smiles began to break across some of the closer creatures' faces. Almost like wildfire, the energy of the few spread quickly throughout the group. Smiles cracked across all sorts of lips, beaks and mauls. Nothing could break the energy in the air. Nothing could sever the tie between this gathered mass. Even when the man on the massive turtle caught a flying tree with his face it did not seem to matter. The chaos was fueling them, pushing them. Each beaming smile and closed set of eyes knew how close it was to finally understanding this great secret.

The smile was contagious. Derek felt his breath racing as his cheeks squeezed in jubilation. He looked at Tella to gauge her own smile, to see her own flurry of excitement, but all he found was a sad face and a shaking head.

"We were so wrong," she said softly. Her voice was barely a whisper, and yet it was the only sound Derek could hear.

In fact, her voice was the only discernable noise. Everything around them had stopped. The trees stood still, the clouds hung loosely. Even the earth was steady. Derek felt his eyes growing heavy. The silence was more threatening than the chaos before it. Slowly, the animals and humans opened their eyes in question. They gathered at the very edge of the void, looking from its depths to each other in question.

"Is it done?" a voice broke through the silence. Derek could not place who said it exactly, but it did not matter. It was the only thought on everyone's mind. Alexander stepped forward and peered into the darkness. Every eye was on him immediately. Both he and the fox on his shoulder shrugged, their silver eyes glistening in merriment.

"Let's see, shall we?" Alexander said, kneeling down and stretching his hand out over the void. The group gasped, watching as the boy's hand passed the level of the ground without a hint of hindrance. Alexander looked over his shoulder to his friends and smiled. His entire face brimmed with pleasure.

When Alexander screamed, though, no one heard it. The sound of the void was too overwhelming. The mile-long hole in the ground had erupted in a gigantic cloud of black and thick, smoldering mist. It shot straight into the sky with a deafening roar, blowing each inquisitive creature back without a second thought. The sound was so thick and wrought with spite it enveloped every thought and feeling in the surrounding area. When Alexander finally yanked back what was left of his arm, the lower half of it was completely disintegrated.

Aden yelled something then as the polar bear and the dark skinned man ran over to help. He dismounted the polar bear and, in one fell swoop, enveloped the fox and the boy in his arms. Over them, the great white bear roared as he spread his paws above his head. The other Tella was already mounted on Gansu, the dragon's wings enveloping everything else. The dragon shot forth a burst of fire into the air. The other Tella stood tall on her dragon's shoulders, catching the fire in her hands. She shot it forward like a shotgun blast, swirling the fire's blaze into a separate whirlwind she had already concocted. Almost as if in response, the thickening mist in front of them shot forward, attacking like a whip. It was useless, though. Each growing tendril only seemed to bounce off the very essence of air and fire. The other Tella turned on her heel, twisting upward with her hands. The fire and whirlwind enveloped her and her friends like a cocoon.

The roaring continued, and Derek could not help but find himself on his knees. He was not exactly hearing the sound. It was more as if he could feel it reverberating deep within his body. Still, he kept his eyes forward. The humans around him who were not quick enough to get up some sort of protection were enveloped by the thickening tendrils of the black mist. One by one, they began to rise into the air, limbs shaking and jerking about, as the entirety of their bodies were being possessed. Every orifice on their horrified bodies now poured forth endless amounts of the thick and darkening mist, their eyes and mouths gaping open. On the ground below them, their animal counterparts lay on the ground, still and deathly silent.

"IT IS TIME FOR THIS AGE TO END."

The voice was not loud, nor was it altogether angry, but it was absolutely controlling. The words tore through each creature from limb to limb. Derek had never been so aware of his shortcomings, of his faults. His spine tingled and his mind wandered. All at once, his face broke into a never-ending smile. He coughed and sputtered, but still the laughter poured forth from within him. Even as death and destruction circled around him, he had never felt so happy. He collapsed to the ground, his legs now jelly. An uncontrollable giggle escaped from within as he rolled around, clutching at his chest. This joy, this feeling! Nothing could compare. His gut wrenched when the tears began to flow. For the first time in his life, he understood sadness. He rolled onto his back and wailed, crying hysterically. Before long, he found himself curled into a little ball. He could barely breathe through the snot pouring from his nose. He tried to sniff it back, to gain control of the never-ending pounding in his chest, but his futility only filled him with rage. He screamed then, pounding himself on the chest. He screamed again, forcing himself onto his knees. Derek felt his vocal cords ripping under the weight of his screams. He shouted nothingness into the void and destruction around him. He wailed his hands against the ground, hammering them until they began to crack and bleed. It was all happening so quickly. He had never felt so out of control.

When Tella could take it no more, she nodded to Caelus and the world around them disappeared into a blank nothingness as the book was yet again enveloped in flame.

Derek allowed himself to breathe. He had no idea what had just happened, no clue about what caused his actions. He lay silent, curled up in the great white expanse. He had never felt so lonely or so vulnerable. Any semblance of usefulness had now washed away into futility. Had he ever felt an emotion before? Honestly, he was no longer sure. An unstoppable flow of tears began to flow down his cheeks. He did not even care to try and stop them.

Tella knelt over him then and placed a hand on his shoulder. It was not much, but it was enough. She knew the feeling all too well. She let Derek gather himself, proud of him then. He sat up bravely enough, though she could still see him trembling. "You were right," he said, the remaining tears glistening in his eyes. "That story was not very fun at all."

"It's also not finished."

Again the book exploded into a rainbow of colors, twisting and forming the white nothingness around them into a dozen different scenes of chaos. "Whatever came out of that void, whatever possessed our friends," Tella said, the pictures of chaos and death swirling over her head, "was simultaneously destroying the world with a darker and deeper understanding than we had ever witnessed." Derek sat on the ground in awe, unable to move. Never before had he witnessed such complete destruction. In each flashing image of the old world, the thick black tower of mist had disappeared, now manifested by the human vessels it had conquered. Each human was stronger than before, even without the help of an animal counterpart. They swirled through the air, flying at breakneck speeds, wreaking havoc on the old world. Mountains were turned to sand and leveled back into the earth from where they had risen. Villages were eradicated by means of tornados, floods, and raging fires. Tsunamis rose from the deepest parts of the oceans, leveling entire coastal regions. Volcano's sprouted from deep within the earth's crust, exploding magma and death upon the surrounding lands. Each wonder was the doing of the possessed and each vessel had the same telltale signs. Every pore and orifice of their bodies oozed with a never-ending amount of the thick and dark mist.

"We watched our friends and families die in front of us," Tella said without hesitation. The vision formed into one solid image then, focusing on a small village in the mountains. The sky turned dark overhead as the clouds died one by one. Over the closest mountaintop, a vessel appeared. No emotion showed on her face. No hint of remorse or lust or happiness. It was worse than that. Her face was nothing more than a blank slate of sheer determination.

"We were completely useless in the end. Nothing we did worked, nothing was effective. We were single-handedly unable to fight and completely unable to do anything to stop its advances." One at a time, the humans and animals of the world tried to band together, to piece together some sort of a resistance. It did not matter in the end. Every result was the exact same. Rarely, whenever a vessel of the mist was actually beaten down, other vessels would show up and put the resistors back in their place.

"What the smoke was allowing the humans to do was unheard of," Tella said as the chaos raged on. "You see, each animal and beast is able to understand the knowledge of the earth and the wind and so forth, but these dark vessels were tapping into something even deeper. Any understanding we thought we had turned out to be nothing in the end. When the first human and animal bonded together, they found that this knowledge could be harnessed to do unfathomable things." A group of polar bears ridden by humans covered in thick wool coats ran across an icy plane. Their faces were complete panic, their motions frantic. It was easy to see that they were running for their lives. Without warning, the ice in front of them melted away in a flash of steam and their entire world was engulfed in flame. Derek was thankful for Tella's narration; otherwise, he knew he would have heard their screams. Three distinct vessels appeared high above the river of fire. Their arms were outstretched and poised, clearly controlling the unending lava below. As dissimilar as each person was in looks, it was almost impossible to miss that they each shared a single daunting trait. Their eyes all swirled with the same pitch black mist.

"We didn't fully understand it," Tella said, the vision around them finally fading away. "We just knew we had to stop it."

"What did you do? I mean, what could you do?" Derek forced himself to keep his view away from his feet.

It was Caelus who finally answered. "It was my ancestors that found the cure for this disease," the dragon boomed. He puffed his chest out in pride.

"What was it?" Derek asked, puffing out his own chest in response. He could not but help match Caelus's energy.

"A knowledge as old and as dark as our own race," the Caelus said. "It was an understanding almost completely forgotten in time, washed away and forbidden. In fact, it was a miracle the oldest of the elders even remembered it, though it was not necessarily for the best." He lowered his head. "This bit of knowledge came with a terrible price."

Derek shielded his eyes as the world around them exploded into a blinding light. Caelus caught Derek's hands with his long and sinewy tail, shaking his head.

"You're not going to want to miss this." The dragon's voice was barely a whisper.

As the light around them took shape, it was easy to see what the dragon meant. The light formed itself into a thousand streams of flowing fire, shooting into the air in every direction. Each fire was endless and plentiful. Each fire was its own shade of blaring heat. Each fire was contained from its own single point, flying towards the middle of the room in a deep and monstrous cavern that continued on for miles in every direction. There was no entrance, no exit; only the endless array of fires spewing forth through the cavern.

And then the source of the fires came into view.

A thousand different dragons lined the walls of the inner mountain. Hunched over and perched perfectly in place, each individual beast roared forth its own fire. The walls around them sparkled and shimmered as the flames caught in each dragon's scale, illuminating their sparkling beauty. Each dragon was like a snowflake, similar and yet completely distinct. No two shared the same color, the same shade. No two shared the same size or weight. Derek realized that he was smiling like an idiot, but he did not care. What boy did not dream of dragons?

The horde of dragons yawned out their flames in near unity. When the fires subsided, all that stood in their place was a deep gray cloud of smoke. The smoke began to dissipate, disappearing into puffs in the air. Floating gently in its place was a mound of molten lava, bubbling and hissing lava onto the ground. It looked like a small sun, forming into its own glorious shape. When the hissing settled, the fire turned to ash and obsidian until cracking like an egg in birth. The ash vanished into the cave's atmosphere.

In its place, now alone and sitting still in the air, was a single and unassuming book.

The other Tella and her friends stood directly underneath it. Alexander patted the fox on his shoulder with his now blackened stump, a remembrance of the darkness they faced. The dark skinned man nodded solemnly to the both of them, the giant polar bear nodding in unison. Each of them looked to the great dragon Gansu, who now stood tall over their group. They were battered and beaten with blood encrusted scars and freshly healing wounds, but still they stood together. The other Tella walked forward, hugging each of her friends in turn. Tears began to pour down her cheeks. Alexander ran to her then, failing to hug her with only his stump of an arm. The fox did not follow. Instead, he had stayed back, his eyes cast dejectedly onto the floor. The dark skinned man separated Alexander and the other Tella gently. He nodded solemnly and lifted his hands into the air, the polar bear echoing his movements. Their faces were as hard as etched stone with not a smile or chuckle to be found.

The cave rang with the sound of the dragon Gansu's roar. Such utter anguish it was. No heart could withstand it. Gansu roared again and attempted to raise his wings to their full glory, but only one rose into the air. The other wing was barely a stem now, a broken stump in its place. He roared for a third time and the other Tella grabbed his face in comfort. She held his beastly snout against her in a failed attempt to calm him. At once, everyone began to sob heavily. Even the burly dark skinned man was beginning to break, his lip quivering as he forced back the tears. Quickly though, as is with all mother figures in a group, the other Tella's resolve returned. Slowly, she stepped forward.

"Please," the other Tella said, her voice echoing through the cavern. "It is time." Her friends knew it was true. In somber response, they each nodded back and slowly formed a circle around her.

Tella stepped forward, watching the scene unfold in front of the book. "We were going to trap this darkness, this *void*, with a knowledge as old as the dragon race could remember. It was, in theory, an understanding more devastating than even it could produce. We had tried before, but nothing we knew of could stick. This time would be different, though."

"Why?" Derek said without hesitation. From what he could tell, nothing the human race or any animal on the earth could produce would ever end in a different result.

"It was simple, really. I'm not sure how we didn't figure it out before." Her eyes were trained on the vision now, burning in a silent fury. "Just like the knowledge itself is stronger and more honed for each beast as it bonds with a human, there is a specific bond that offers a link so powerful that nothing can touch it or best it. It is an ancient and messy thing, and it requires the most brutal of sacrifices."

Derek gritted his teeth, the scene before him finally beginning to click. He knew the answer almost immediately.

Tella smiled at him then, proud yet again. "It is the bond of life itself."

Her old circle of friends lifted their respective arms in response, lifting the other Tella gently into the air on the lightest of winds. Up and up she went, until stopping directly next to the newly formed book. The other Tella nodded to her friends.

In one last and finite cry, Gansu roared in command. A deep and murky fire exploded from his throat, enveloping both the other Tella and the book floating next to her. It was a twisting and perfect stream of lava that hung around her, dancing and twirling in the air. Gansu's single stream soon exploded into a cascade of fire as the cavern of dragons added their own shades of breath into the mix. The other Tella was engulfed instantly. Derek was glad it happened quickly for he could not bear the screaming and searing pain that flashed across the other Tella's face, right before she gave one last glance to her group of friends.

After what seemed like an eternity, the fires subdued and the ash and steam settled. When the smog cleared, only the book stood floating in place. No other Tella accompanied it. Any trace of the once beautiful girl had now completely vanished. The atmosphere was thick with silence. The seconds rolled along, and uncertainty began to set in. Nothing seemed to happen. Murmurs of wasted breath began to break the eerie quiet, but they were quickly silenced when a soft, pulsating light began to emit from deep within the book's pages.

A smile crept across Derek's lips. The book had begun to glow.

The world in front of them flashed yet again, the vision changing pace. Derek did not even close his eyes this time, he only let them sting with joy. When the colors settled, Derek knew where he was instantly; where this madness all began.

The world around them was a desolate wasteland, completely void of the monstrous trees it once held. All types of vegetation and grass had withered, leaving only clumps of rotted earth in its place. Derek walked around, looking as far as he could see, though everything was the same.

The only thing that stood unchanged was the gigantic void that stretched across the earth.

"We had the plan and the tools now," Tella said, walking up beside Derek. The book floated over her shoulder. "Next, we just needed to lure out the beast itself." Her gaze shifted to the sky above.

The sun vanished immediately. In its place, a dark and luminous cloud began to fill the air. It blocked almost the entire sky from view, accompanied by a low and humming sound. The sound grew and grew and the cloud came into view. From every direction, the sky had exploded into a thick mass of beating wings. As if in response, the earth began to shake. Off in the distance, tall and looming shapes began to peak over the horizon with only dust following in their wake. It seemed that every type of beast, bird, human and creature left alive in the world was gathering now at the heart of it all.

Without warning, the void exploded into a tornado of the same thick, dark mist. A deep yet shrill note pierced Derek's ears, forcing him to cover them with his hands. He fought the urge to cry, the urge to drop to his knees and whimper. The void's human vessels began to burst from within the smoke like banshees, dispersing instantly into the gathering crowds of animals and humans. Fire, lightning, wind and earth came crashing down upon them in an instant as they threw everything they had at each other. From above, whirlwinds and tornados formed and met with vanishing icebergs and walls of fire. From below, the earth split in every direction, small mountains being formed and destroyed in unison as the war waged on. The chaos thickened, and the only thing that was certain was the growing number of voices crying out in pain. After what felt like an eternity, the massive hole in the ground sat still again, the cloud of darkness finally reaching its end. Every particle of it was now joined in the fight at its gates. The animals and their human counterparts stood no chance though. It was only a matter of time until they were completely wiped out.

"Do you notice a pattern, Derek?" Tella said, their view of the battlefield changing to overhead.

He looked down. The vessels tore through the ranks of animals, but death and destruction was all that was registering. His brow furrowed in frustration. "I don't notice a thing," he said at first, but the moment the words left his lips, he knew he spoke too soon. Slowly, he began to realize that the animals sacrificing themselves were doing so in complete synchronization. There was a method to their madness, a specific and meticulously planned out strategy. On the other side of the battlefield, more than a mile away from the actual chaos, a looming mist stood in place. Perfectly white and thinner than the air itself, the mist was barely a shimmering on the horizon. He turned his attention back to the battlefield and began to nod to himself as the plan took shape in his head.

Then he noticed what was missing from the battle.

"The dragons are in the mist," Derek said, the words almost catching in his throat.

Tella beamed in response.

With one last and final surge, every bonded creature lashed out and forced the vessels together into one spot, directly below the mist. The vessels hesitated, wondering what the next move would be, but it was too late. The mist dissipated, revealing thousands of dragons hovering in a perfect star shaped formation. Each dragon was accompanied by a human of no specific race or gender, with one hand to their heart and another placed gently on a dragon's head. Together, they began to chant. The earth shivered from its core and each dragon raised its head, roaring to the heavens above. In a flash of light and stars and sun and moon, the entire sky seemed to light up with a power the likes of which the planet had never witnessed. Each vessel's body jerked rigidly, caught in the cosmic entrapment. The sky overhead began to turn a deep turquoise as it was filled with an energy as old as the beginning of life.

The trap had worked and the vessels were gathered within the dragon's formation. Their bodies were locked in unison, heads cocked backwards in rigid positions. They raged in silence, their mouths moving as if screaming but with no sound escaping. Thick and dark mist shot from their mouths, from their ears, from their pores, only to rescind as if blocked by some invisible wall of energy.

From deep within the formation of dragons, Tella's group stepped out onto the battlefield. The dark skinned man and his polar bear, the dragon Gansu and even the small boy with his fox were all visible, shaking with determination. Gansu's head swiveled upwards. In response a glowing book floated over the dragon's remaining wing. The friends looked at each other and nodded, lifting their spirits towards the enraged vessels. Gansu lifted his wing in triumph and enveloped the book in flame.

The earth split directly down the middle with a groan. It was neither a shaking nor a sound of cracking under strain; it was the sound of the ground breaking at its very foundation. The vessels began to shake in response. Derek was pleased. They looked absolutely terrified.

The vision changed again, this time to the original view of the earth. The land below shook and the oceans trembled. Piece by piece, the gigantic continent began to split and fragment into pieces.

"So you really did break the world," Derek said, his eyes glued to the ages passing in a flash below. The continents shifted, the seas churned, the earth froze over time and time again as the lands took shape. The clouds disappeared, the water recessed and flooded. Over time, the pieces of the continent settled into place until forming what looked like the beginning of the earth Derek called home.

He looked up, finding Tella and Caelus standing directly behind him. "What happened with the death cloud thing?"

"We trapped it," Tella answered. "With the strength of the dragons channeled through my sacrifice, we were able to rip the death cloud thing, as you put it, from its human forms and eradicate the majority of its presence." Tella frowned. "Though, we could not eradicate all of it." She shook her head and sighed. "Little did we know that the cost of such knowledge could destroy the world."

"Destroy?" Derek asked. "What do you mean, destroy?"

"The earth died that day, Derek," she said without hesitation, walking out into the air and observing the changing lands below. "It died and it cost the energy of every living dragon to keep it turning."

Derek looked to Caelus, noticing the shifting in the great beast's expression. His wings drooped now, his head following suit. It was like a great and terrible burden had just been placed on the creature, one that Derek knew he could not understand.

Tella caught Derek's eyes and nodded. "Caelus is currently the last of the dragon kind," she said softly. "Both his race's sacrifice and mine are the only thing that keeps the world turning."

"How?" Derek said, walking up beside her. He looked into her eyes and was surprised to find that not a hint of sadness remained. Instead, her normal steely resolve sat firmly in place.

Tella gestured softly out over the earth, her hand a soft and simple wave. "The world itself is sustained through our knowledge and our bond. One dragon and one girl, captured in the fire and flame of its race." Tella turned toward Caelus and rested a hand on his head. "You see, Derek, the dragons used their race to save the world, to keep it turning, to keep it alive. They molded each breath they would ever take as a being into a single egg, entrusted to the one dragon living at the time. It is the cycle that sustains the world."

"One dragon and its egg to keep the world on its legs, the cycle must continue," Caelus said with grunt. Derek and Tella winced at the rhyme in unison. Caelus huffed. "Well, I didn't write it. Blame my great, great grand dragon!" Caelus lowered his head, murmuring under his breath.

"One dragon, one egg and me to guide it," Tella said, ignoring the dragon. "When it comes time, Caelus will pass on and the new dragon will find me waiting to teach it the burden of its race."

"So when Caelus dies," Derek began, ignoring the huff of indignation the dragon gave at the thought, "will the new egg just hatch? Where do the eggs come from?"

"It is a self sustaining cycle," Tella said. "The dragon passes, the new is born, carrying with it the next egg. Both are raised to be protector and understand their importance."

"So male dragons have eggs, too? Like a seahorse?"

Caelus scoffed. "A *what?*"

Derek shrugged. "You know, a seahorse."

The dragon stared in disbelief. "I am no swimming horse!"

Tella raised her hands, quieting down the both of them. "Each dragon is birthed from a specific lineage, a race once remembered," she continued. "They do not *carry* a new egg inside of them, so much as they're born with it. Or next to it, to be exact."

"That is weird," Derek laughed to himself.

Tella's eyes twinkled. "*Magic.*"

Derek nodded and looked out over the still changing earth. Behind him, he could still hear Caelus murmuring to himself. He breathed deeply and chuckled, surprised that this information overload did not in fact surprise him. In truth, it was rather easy to accept. The world he had known was boring and unfulfilling. What kid would not want to live in a crazy and magical land with dragons and magic and talking cats?

He bit his lip as the thought caught in his brain. *Talking cats indeed.* He frowned and shook his head in remission.

"What's wrong?" Tella asked.

"Nothing I guess," he shrugged. "It's just weird to know you've been lied to."

Both Tella and Caelus turned immediately, but Derek did not notice. Instead, he only chuckled to himself at his own stupidity.

"What do you mean *lied to?*" Caelus asked. His tone was deeper now, any hint of playfulness completely vanished.

"No, no, it's nothing," Derek said peering over the earth with a sigh. "It's just that the cat said he wrote the book and that the dragon was evil and trying to destroy the world. To think, I actually believed that the book had chosen me to be the world's savior!" He slapped himself on the forehead, laughing at his own stupidity.

"What cat?" Tella's asked softly. The tone broke through Derek's rambling in an instant.

He stopped, taken aback. When had Caelus come over to him? Derek looked at Tella's face, but was only met with her singular look of determination. He cleared his throat but found no voice. When had they both become so intimidating?

"She asked you a question, Derek," the dragon rumbled deep within his chest. "What cat?"

"You know, the cat," Derek said defensively. "The one who brought us here!" He pointed at Tella and then himself. This time, Derek did catch the look that flashed between the girl and her dragon.

"Derek, I'm the one who brought you here," Tella said coldly. Each word was meticulously placed. "There was no cat."

"What are you talking about?" Derek said with his hands, waving them as if it would help his case. It did not seem to. "The cat was with us the whole time," he said frantically. "He showed me how to use the book, he saved us from the wolves, he even gave me Prometheus's gun!"

The silence that followed was icy and rigid. Caelus sat back on his haunches, shaking his massive head. "Oh, Derek," Tella said, the deep sadness returning to her eyes one vanishing sparkle at a time. "You silly, silly boy." She stood, turning toward Caelus in a flurry. "We need to return."

"Why? What did I do?" Derek stood and followed.

"You've done nothing yet," she said in response, laying her hand on the dragon's head. "But, we just need to keep it that way." She nodded to Caelus. "Let's go."

Caelus nodded back and filled his lungs with fire, but it was too late. With a sickening thud, the dragon's skull burst into a flurry of scale, flesh and blood as the bullet exploded out of the other side. Derek dropped to his knees, his stomach reeling. The sound of the gunshot rang endlessly in his ears as the world around them was ripped from his conscious mind.

CHAPTER TWELVE

When Derek came to he immediately loosened whatever substances his stomach still carried onto the ground. The sunlight, the *real* sunlight and not just a vision of it within himself, stung his eyes instantly. He attempted to blink away the tears, to force them back so that he could see, but to no avail. His ears still rang, his head was still spinning. The surrounding area was quiet, too quiet, though he doubted he could hear anything past the high pitched ringing in his ears. Leg by leg he tried to stand, but instead he only fell to the ground screaming. He had forgotten about his broken ankle. The moment he put his weight on it the ankle twisted and buckled beneath him. He fumbled around on the ground, his hands clawing at the dirt. Regaining his composure seemed impossible. He tried to calm himself, to steady his breathing, but he could not shake the feeling that he would never make sense of what just happened.

The memory of the bullet passing through Caelus's skull was disgustingly detailed and his brain would not stop playing it on repeat.

The first thing to return was his hearing, though in all honesty he wished it had not. When the high pitched squeal in his ears finally subsided, a shrill and boisterous cackle was all that was left. Derek would rather have stayed deaf the rest of his life than ever hear that laugh again. He opened his eyes, forcing them to adjust to the blinding sun as he wiped away the tears.

The harsh and piercing laugh continued. Slowly, ever so slowly, the shapes around him began to register in his mind. He was at the mouth of the dragon's cave, lying immobile on the ground. The cave itself was dark and empty, almost ominous. He looked down and felt the weight of the book in his lap. It was lying open now, empty of any glow. It looked like nothing more than a book with blank pages.

Derek forced his gazed upwards. Not six feet away, Caelus lay on the ground, his body a lifeless lump. Blood poured from the hole in his skull out onto the ground. Tears stung Derek's eyes and he knew they were not from the sun. He had wished and hoped that the last part of the vision was a trick or maybe a cruel joke. It was not. The dragon was dead.

Another round of cackling broke through his thoughts, and the incessant noise began to register as actual words. Derek's entire stomach dropped out again as he realized who now stood laughing and dancing joyfully over the dragon's carcass. There, without any explanation or any reason, stood Professor Prometheus. The old man laughed and hooted his way around the newly departed dragon, waving his trusty revolver in the air over his head.

"I did it. I did it, I did!" Prometheus screamed in an almost singsong manner. He danced and jigged his way around the carcass before laying his head upon the dead dragon's body with a begrudging smile. "I am a dragon slayer. I am a slayer of decades and history and all the world shall know!" Prometheus hugged the dragon's carcass, tears streaming down his face. "Thank you, dear dragon. Thank you for everything, you fantastic lump of meat. You have single-handedly made me the greatest human ever known!"

Derek wiped his mouth as the man in front of him ranted and raved, his brain only now beginning to take in exactly how terrible Prometheus looked. His arms were scarred from shoulder to fingertips, blood caked over them from side to side. His khakis were covered in layers of mud and filth. The once beautiful and flowing beard was scattered like a wild mane below his maniacal eyes. Every wrinkle on Prometheus's face was chiseled and hardened, etched there by centuries of scowling. Where was the great and gentle explorer he had met? Derek gagged at the sight and immediately regretted it.

Prometheus had finally noticed him.

"Derek, my boy. You've come to!" Prometheus said with a laugh, falling off the dragon's body. "My ass," he said, rubbing himself. "How silly of me!" He stood then, wiping himself off as he began to prance toward Derek. "Do you see what I've done? Do you see what I've found? I killed a dragon, Derek. A *dragon!*" He danced around Derek in a circle, pointing to the great beast. "I am not crazy. They will see I am not crazy!" He shouted then and hollered nonsense into the air before bending down and enveloping Derek in a strange and arduous hug. "I don't know how you did it, but I have to thank you. I know that the little bastard feline hid my house, but never had I guessed that you were with him. I thought my little beauty was lost forever." He held out his gun, his eyes welling in endearment. "How I have missed this little hunk of metal." He put the gun to his lips and kissed it.

"Thank you, Derek," Prometheus said warmly. "Thank you, thank you, thank you! I cannot say it enough." Prometheus knelt down in front of him, a wide and teary smile etched across his face. "Sincerely boy, you have let me etch my name in history. If it was not for you or that backstabbing little kitty, I never would have gotten the drop on this wretched beast so perfectly."

Prometheus stood, his face growing darker. He walked stealthily over to the dragon, like he was afraid it would suddenly awake. "Oh, I've thought about it, fantasized about it," he said, laying himself along its belly. He stroked each scale longingly with his gun. Derek did not have to guess that Prometheus was enjoying his handiwork. It repulsed him that the crazed man was reveling in it.

"Dragons are a *myth*, Prometheus! They do not *exist*, Prometheus!" he screamed, spittle spewing from his lips. *"Magic is not real, Prometheus!"* He spat onto the ground and stood up straight. He took one long breath and looked back to the poor boy sitting by his lonesome. A smile broke across his lips, so perfect and white. "But they were wrong, weren't they Derek?" His voice was barely a whisper, his eyes sunken and deep. "They were wrong, *and I proved them wrong.*"

Derek sat up, grabbing the book and opening it in his lap. Nothing. No glow, no response. He flipped through the pages, praying for help, for anything. He could feel his heart thudding in his stomach.

"You were reading it, weren't you?" Prometheus stood over him now, his eyes barely visible slits as he scowled at the book. "You were actually *reading* it!" Prometheus yanked the book from Derek's lap before he had a chance to react. The boy tried to fight, tried to take it back, but the pain from his ankle overtook him.

"You miserable little creature!" Prometheus screamed, shaking the book violently. He tried to rip at the pages, but they would not budge. He screamed again, throwing the book at Derek's face. "*Why!?* What did I do wrong? Why was I not good enough to discover its mysteries!?" Prometheus loomed over Derek, the gun shaking in both of his hands. The old man's eyes were enraged, popping directly out of his head. "I should have been the one, *boy!* Me!" Prometheus screamed. He squeezed the gun's handle harder and harder, forcing each vein in his arms to throb. "It should have been me! Why was it not me?!"

Derek covered his face with the book, knowing this was how it would end. At least with a bullet it would be over quickly. This, of course, is an extremely sobering thought for any fifteen-year-old boy, but such is to be expected when facing death. His ears hummed with a deep and low vibration. His heart pounded in his chest and throat. He let them pass, waiting patiently for his end to come. Tears welled yet again in his eyes and he knew if he had anything left in his stomach he probably would have thrown it up. Such a waste was his life, to end like this, but what could be done? He gulped and readied himself, apologizing to his mother and siblings in his head for not being there, for not doing enough. The pounding in his chest increased, thumping loudly. He knew he was not exactly ready to die, but he resolved himself to his fate.

The bullet never came. Derek lowered the book in confusion. It was then he noticed that the throbbing in his chest was abnormal, as was the buzzing in his skull. It was then he realized that he had felt this feeling before. In fact, he knew it all too well. This feeling had been growing inside of him the whole time, filling his being. His head jerked to the mouth of the cave and his vision blurred in answer.

It was then he knew that he was too late.

Derek began to laugh uncontrollably. The sound was genuine, though the feelings were not. He could not help it. He doubled over and felt his stomach contract again and again as the sound filled his body. He was so happy, so blissfully unaware of his surroundings that it filled him with joy. A giggle burst from his lips and he hoped the feeling would never end. That was, until the sadness came. His heart broke into a million pieces and the tears raced like a flood down his cheeks. How severe and terrible his life had been. There would be no answer, there would be no resolve. It was all meaningless. He screamed, filling with an unquenchable rage as he began to pound the earth with his fists. His palms cracked and bled under the attack, but it did not matter. No life was worth it. No feelings were worth it. There was nothing that would help.

Through the thick fog of his emotions, he forced himself to look up. Prometheus's back was turned to Derek now, his attention drawn toward the cave. Why was he not writhing on the ground? How could he just stand there, so still and so upright? It was like some unknown force had overtaken Prometheus's entire body. Derek tried to shout, to yell, anything to distract the rigid old man, but nothing came out. His head throbbed and his vision dissolved into a milky hue. He forced himself to breathe. The noise was vibrating in his ribcage so hard that it was becoming more difficult.

"I NEED A VESSEL."

All at once, the throbbing stopped. Derek coughed and spat, wiping his vision clean. He shook his head and looked again at the mouth of the cave.

A small black cloud of thick and ever darkening mist floated out from within.

"I NEED A VESSEL."

The words repeated, this time exploding in Derek's mind. Tears welled in his eyes, but he knew these were not from any forced emotion. These tears were real. These tears were the result of fear. He looked up and froze. The little black cloud of mist was floating directly over him. He could not explain it, but he knew the little cloud was staring at him, weighing his very existence. After a moment the mist turned and floated away, rejecting him outright. Derek had never felt so meaningless.

"YOU ARE NOT MY VESSEL."

The words shook Derek to the core. The small cloud of swirling dark and dust turned its attention on Prometheus then, floating over to the petrified old man. The mist probed at him, poking his every joint and muscle with black and sinewy tendrils. From head to toe he was probed. Piece by piece, he too was weighed.

"PERFECTION."

The cloud breathed in, taking the surrounding air with it. After a moment it exhaled, expanding ten times its normal size. Prometheus did not even twitch when his body became enveloped; he only tilted his head back and opened his mouth in welcome. The mist poured into the old man's lungs, causing him to hack and cough until they were filled. Each vein in Prometheus's body began to swirl in color. They changed from yellow to brown, from a dark and sickly green to a bright purple, until they swelled with a deep and charcoal black, pulsing audibly. His eyes were the last to change. They rolled back in agony and despair as the life flickered out of them, exploding with a thick black mist. The little cloud had disappeared completely within Prometheus's body.

When the transformation ended, Prometheus landed on the ground without a single noise. His slightly arched back popped and cracked as he stood up straight. He looked at himself then, inspecting the individual elements of his body. Starting at his fingers, he began to flex each muscle and joint in his hands until he moved on to his arms. One by one, his scars reopened with a crackling sound. Little black particles of darkness rose from within and evaporated into the air. He went on to his back and torso, flexing as if to get a feel for his own pale and ghostly skin. Prometheus nodded to himself and his eyes flickered with a dull and lifeless shine, marred only by the ever present darkness swirling within them.

"I am weak," he said finitely. The voice croaked and groaned as it filtered out in a low yet fierce boom. It was a strange admission coming from such an otherworldly being, but after seeing what the void could do in its prime, Derek was relieved to hear it.

Prometheus began to check his surroundings, his blackened pupils scanning every inch around him. He looked from the dragon's carcass to the gun lying on the ground, then to the cave opening and the sky blaring overhead. Lastly, his attention turned to Derek. Their eyes met and Prometheus's pitch-black pupils twisted in recognition.

"The mind inside this body seems to think that you are to thank for my rebirth," Prometheus said in his low and now thriving voice. The void began to walk in his direction, his feet not making a sound. Derek tried to move, to roll over onto his back and crawl away, but his limbs did not respond. He only sat there immobilized and trembling. The void knelt down next to him. Derek barely had time to blink before Prometheus tilted his head in both question and answer.

"You are hurt." Derek winced as Prometheus reached out and touched his broken ankle with a single fingertip. Black mist crawled forth, slithering around Derek's foot. Again the boy tried to squirm, to move away, but his body was overwhelmed with every sensation that the human psyche could handle. Hatred boiled into laughter deep in his stomach, then into madness, sadness and envy. His body shook uncontrollably under the weight, his stomach contracting again and again until eventually he screamed.

"At the end of this age, know that I am not unjust," Prometheus said, standing and retracting his touch. Derek gasped for air and his mind settled in a jolt. He looked down at his ankle, knowing that it had been healed. Never had he felt so powerless, so innocent. He probed at it with his thumb and then began to sob.

When he finally looked up, he found Prometheus standing still, inspecting a floating object in front of him. Mist rose again from Prometheus's outstretched fingers, and the object began to glow.

Derek gasped. "No! You can't!" He reached out as he screamed. When had Prometheus grabbed the book? His heart beat like a drum in his chest.

Prometheus silenced him with a single glance. "You are not my equal," he said quietly. "You will never command me again." Without a second thought, he turned his attention back to the floating book in front of him. He raised a hand to his chin, his head cocked in what seemed like veiled curiosity. He probed and prodded, touching the book in different spots on its leather binding and pages, causing the book to shimmer with each stroke.

"I see now why I was defeated." He reached out a finger and rubbed the book down the inside of its spine. Instantly, the book shuddered, exploding in a flurry of light despite itself. Prometheus's face darkened, the scars on his arm pulsing with the dark mist. He held his palm out over the trembling manuscript and yanked back with all of his might.

Tella's scream sent shivers down Derek's spine. He tried again to shout something, anything to distract Prometheus, but his voice only croaked. He could only sit and watch Tella fall to the ground in front of him, her body bent over, completely dejected. She rose to her elbows. Derek had never seen her look so feeble. She began to crawl her way over to Caelus's body, draping herself over her old friend. Derek was not surprised to find she held her tears at bay. When she finally made eye contact with Derek, it was not hate he found in her eyes but a severe and crushing loneliness.

"This is my great undoing?" Prometheus asked. He watched curiously, his head held lightly to the side. He walked purposefully over to Tella, before crouching barely an inch from her face. He held out a hand and caressed her chin. "You are but a girl. A small, insignificant human girl. To think that such a sacrifice would be the catalyst for my defeat." Prometheus began to laugh. It was not the shrill, crazed laugh of the original Prometheus, though Derek wished that it was. This new laugh was barely more than a chuckle, a soothing and evocative baritone.

Tella's eyes darted to the book and then back to her own body. She pressed her hand against her face. "Am I alive?" she said coolly, keeping her voice even.

"Oh, how I wish girl," Prometheus said as the laughter subdued. "If you were anything more than an illusion, I would torture you past the end of all the ages for what you have done to me." Prometheus stood and plucked the book out of the air. His smile vanished, his face darkening. He raised his palm again, his arms pulsing with the dark mist. He turned it on the book and formed both of his hands in a circular fashion.

"I just wanted a chance to see your face before I erase it from memory," Prometheus said with a single, gratified smile.

A cat with fur as cold and haunting as the hovering night landed lightly on Prometheus's head. The cat licked his paw casually, letting his tail flick from side to side in beat with some internal metronome. The world seemed silent, almost hesitant, like it was unsure about how to react. For a brief second, surely no longer than a mere blink, Derek caught the twinkle in the cat's eyes as they made contact with his own.

When the cat leaped from his perch, Prometheus's head exploded in a bold blue flame. Prometheus shrieked, releasing the book from whatever spell he had it held in. Time seemed to slow as the cat landed on a small tuft of wind, catching the book on his awaiting back. Three small, self-contained tornados began to swirl under the cat before they exploded. The cat turned on his paw, and both he and the book were shot toward Derek like a rocket. He flipped in the air gracefully before landing and letting the book fall lightly into Derek's lap.

"Close the book, Derek," the cat said, his voice too relaxed for the situation.

"Where the hell have you been?" Derek asked. His heart was racing, but he could not tell if it was from rage, hope or some other new and unknown emotion. Honestly, he was not sure if he cared.

"There isn't time for that," the cat said, his tone quick and precise. The cat's stare was trained on Prometheus, whose head was still writhing in flame. "Now, *close the book, Derek.*"

Derek grabbed the book from his lap and caught Tella's eyes. Their stare seemed to hold for an eternity. "Thank you," she mouthed. Derek closed the book with a nod and Tella fizzled out of sight.

Derek stood and tucked the book under his arm. He turned to the cat, awaiting the feline's next move. The cat said nothing. He only stared at Prometheus, his tail swaying methodically behind him. It was not long before the dark mist exploded from within the man, extinguishing the fire in a dark and yet luminous cloud. Prometheus stood with his eyes bulging. Unsurprisingly, he had come out completely unscathed. He turned on the cat then and steadied his breathing.

"Stay here," the cat said to Derek coolly. How could he be so collected? The cat stretched his back with a shrug. Derek was almost a bit jealous of the cat's casual attitude.

"What are you going to do?" Derek asked, failing miserably to match the cat's tone.

"Don't ask silly questions," the cat said with a smile. "I've taught you better than that."

Prometheus cracked his neck and knuckles, offering himself a deep and well-placed breath. He began to walk towards them methodically.

"Okay, that's nice," Derek said, the worry cracking his voice as it came out. "I'm pretty sure that thing is going to destroy you, though."

The cat smiled ruefully. "I like my odds."

"Odds? What odds?" Derek said, waving his open hand. "There aren't any odds!"

The cat shrugged. "I have more lives left than him. So, I like my odds." For as playful as his voice sounded, Derek could see that the cat's piercing gaze never left Prometheus's direction.

"YOU FEARFUL AND STUPID CREATURES."

Prometheus's voice boomed in their skulls, reverberating against each inner wall. Both Derek and the cat stood at the ready. Prometheus steadied his breathing, calming his voice down. He pierced the cat with his icy gaze. "You do not know who you trifle with."

The cat chuckled. "Well, personally, and I could be wrong about this," the cat said as he began to pace his way away from Derek. "I see a cowering little piece of dark mist hiding inside the skin of a very disturbed human." The cat's legs were relaxed, its entire body seemingly loose. Derek knew better, though. By the way the cat's tail flicked methodically from side to side, it was clear how seriously he took the situation at hand.

"Do you like humans?" the cat asked, stepping closer to Prometheus. "I don't. They're pushy for one, and for two the older they are the more they tend to smell. I can only imagine what it's like to be inside one's skin. It makes me want to vomit." The cat shuddered, gagging on his own words. Prometheus's face was void of emotion. Step by step, the two closed the ground between them.

"Then again, it doesn't surprise me," the cat continued. "You are such a wretched little piece of knowledge. It is only fitting that you would hide inside such a vile excuse for a man. Can he hear me? Does he know how much I loathe him?" The cat shrugged again. "It makes sense, though. You two seem almost made for each other. You're both cowards."

In the blink of an eye, Prometheus was no longer in front of the cat. Instead, he was behind him with his hands outstretched and waiting. He closed his fingers and instantly his scars erupted in the dark mist, racing toward the cat with a blinding speed. The cat tried to turn, to twist around, but it was too late. He was enveloped completely, his body squirming and jerking the moment it came in contact with the mist. The cat hissed and spat and his body began to writhe in pain.

"I mean, I get it, you think you're all powerful." The cat's voice rang from the opposite side of the clearing. Derek looked back at Prometheus, pleased to see he was as shocked as Derek. They both looked to where the cat sat now, licking a paw indifferently. The mist in front of Prometheus exploded in a flurry of the cat's signature deep blue flame, evaporating into nothingness.

"What I don't get, and try to follow me on this," the cat said, beginning to pace his way back to Prometheus. "If you're this all powerful dark substance, why the need for such an atrocious human vessel? You would think such a high and mighty power could do something without the need for man."

The mist began to swirl furiously inside Prometheus's jet black eyes. Was this a sign of anger, an actual emotion? Prometheus raised his hand again, this time sending a lightning bolt crashing to the ground. The cat was enveloped in the electricity, his body evaporating with a sizzle, but again the cat appeared on the other side of Prometheus, unharmed and unscathed.

"Do you see the rest of us pilfering human bodies?" the cat asked, almost hurt. "Of course not. That's gross and even a little disturbing. It really brings in to question the validity of your claims." He shook his head gingerly. "Quite frankly, it makes you seem a bit desperate."

Deep black balls of fire began to pour forth from Prometheus's outstretched hand as he shot one after another to where the cat supposedly was. "Come now, this is just pitiful!" the cat said, disappearing again and again around the clearing. Once or twice the cat would allow himself to be hit, shrieking with rage and screams of death, only to reappear on another side of the clearing with a chuckle.

"I'm disappointed," the cat said as the barrage ended. He shook his head and placed a paw on his chest as if soaked to the core in hurt. "The human you possessed was more powerful than you! At least he could take down a dragon."

Prometheus stood straight and at the ready, no longer focused on where exactly the cat was sitting. Instead, he lowered his eyes and just stared at his feet as if sensing every element of the surrounding area.

The cat arched his back, his voice quieting. "It looks to me like you should have stayed in that jar."

It was barely a whisper, but it was more enough. Prometheus's head jerked up in reaction, his attention landing on the dragon's carcass with a smile. "Your illusions grow tiresome," he said, hunching over. He breathed in, relaxing each muscle in his human body. Darkness began to ooze out of every pore. Panic flashed across the cat's face.

Prometheus twirled on his heel, pointing his palm toward Caelus's carcass. The mist shot forward in a flurry. The dragon's body vanished completely, leaving only the cat sitting alone. The illusion was shattered. On the opposite side of the clearing, the dragon's actual body lay alone and unhindered. The cat was caught in the dark mist, rising into the air with a shriek.

Prometheus walked over, his face still lacking of emotion. He studied the cat from limb to limb, testing his every inch for secrets. Prometheus sniffed, an eyebrow raised at a sudden thought. "You have a lifeless air about you, animal." For once, his face broke into an emotion of curiosity. "It seems death as it is known in this realm holds no limit over you. What sort of atrocity must an animal commit to gain such power?" Prometheus shrugged then, letting the emotions wash through him. "It is very curious, but nothing is absolutely certain. Your remaining lives shall be extinguished one by one."

The cat hissed venomously.

Prometheus turned on his heel, reaching a hand out to the book again. He let the cat squirm helplessly in the air as the mist gripped the feline's body. Black and endless tendrils gushed forward, filling the cat's mouth, ears and nose. The cat gagged and wheezed on thickening smoke as every bit of air evaporated from within. The gargling noise could only be cat's attempt to scream. His body went limp and the fight was extinguished from him. His eyes rolled into the back of his head. It was a finite feeling that Derek had in his chest. He knew he had just watched the cat die for the second time in his own life.

Prometheus lifted the book in his hands, opening it methodically. Derek looked down to his lap in surprise, not knowing when Prometheus had even grabbed the book in the first place, but he knew he would have been powerless to stop him. Prometheus lifted a finger to the book, about to caress its spine and again rip Tella from within, but he was interrupted when the sound of coughing began. The cat spat, hissed and hacked his way back to life, his head shaking violently as if taking the brunt of the action for his immoveable body.

"I will destroy you!" the cat screamed, his lifeless pupils filling with recognition. His gaze immediately went to Prometheus, knowing exactly where he would be. Every inch of his fur was bristling in the mist. His entire body seemed to be filled with a kinetic energy urging to be released. "I will eviscerate your being, unraveling you from the core of whatever knowledge you think keeps you safe!" The cat screamed and screamed, his rage building. His eyes were but determined slits, his voice final. Prometheus watched silently, unhindered by the threats.

"You are nothing to me, you little blight!" the cat continued, hissing with a visceral rage, spewing out each syllable. "You are leftovers from a dead age, an emptiness barely worth a child's nightmares! You are a mere nothingness of decadent filth hiding inside a putrid man's skin. I will—"

The mist shot forth from Prometheus's outstretched hand. He said nothing as again the black substance filled the cat's mouth and lungs. This time was different, though. This time, the cat made neither a sound nor a squeal. Instead, he only stared defiantly at Prometheus until eventually his pupils and head rolled back into a lifeless slump. Prometheus watched the cat die, clinching his jaw in a small allowance of adoration. He closed the book and walked over to the cat's lifeless body, watching as the cat's tongue rolled out of his mouth. Placing the book neatly under his arm, Prometheus waited patiently for the cat to return.

Eventually, when the cat did return, he returned not with a convulsing or a shaking. Instead, as the life filled his pupils, the cat sat up perfectly calm and deathly quiet. His eyes focused purely on Prometheus, not surprised in the least that he was now standing so close.

"—I will follow you into the depths of whatever hell that spawned you," the cat whispered. "If not today, if not tomorrow, I will be your end in whichever age you find yourself in. This I promise."

Prometheus let the cat's words hang in the air. The cat knew that the being inside his late partner was judging him for everything the cat was, but it did not bother him. At that moment the cat's nose twitched. Could it be? He dared not hope. His nose twitched again as the scent caught for a second time. Had the black mist caught it too? From the way Prometheus stared at him now, the cat knew he had not. The mist had been in that jar for too long, it did not know the air and the taste of the trees like the cat did. He kept his eyes trained on Prometheus, not letting a single hint of hope shine through.

"You know your struggle is futile and yet you still persist," Prometheus said, entirely unaware. He only cocked his head to the side in curiosity. He did not show sorrow or emotion, just a slight bewilderment. "I do not understand why your kind always clings so heavily to its feeble existence."

The cat smirked. "That is because you are an idiot."

The lightning that struck was quick and brutal, but the cat was ready. In a flash, Prometheus was enveloped in the thunderbolt that descended from above. The cat allowed himself a brief moment of satisfaction. He watched Prometheus's skin crackle underneath the massive weight of the electricity, melting bone and skin. As soon as the lightning hit, the mist began to fill the wounds on his face. The skin rescinded, flesh melting under the heat, but the mist healed its vessel even quicker. The cat took everything in, making mental notes it would not soon forget.

The mist loosened around the cat's body. It was not much, but even the slightest give was enough. In a split second, the cat breathed in heavily, loosened his spine and let forth a gigantic bale of the blue flame directly in Prometheus's face. His arms shot up, mist pouring out in droves from deep in his being. A cloud of darkness solidified itself around Prometheus then, creating an almost protective aura as the book dropped from his grip. The cat dropped to the ground, twisting and catching the book in his mouth. After another deep breath the cat felt the air catch his paw, before exploding and propelling the book forth in a tumultuous gust of wind.

Without a second to spare, Derek caught the book from the cat's mouth as the feline flipped and twisted, landing next to him in one smooth motion. He tucked the book under his arm protectively.

Never again would he lose it while he still held breath. Never again would he sit and do nothing, even when there was nothing he could do.

Derek looked at Prometheus, knowing what troubles lay in front of him. He flashed the cat a rueful grin. "I don't know what the hell you just did, but thank god you did it."

"I didn't do a single thing," the cat said, matching Derek's smirk with his own. He nodded to the treetops. "They did."

The leaves began to shudder individually, each shimmering with a bushy tail. *Squirrels.* One by one, the squirrels began to hop from branch to branch in a clockwork circle around the clearing. They chattered amongst themselves, their teeth clicking and clacking in perfect harmony. Derek squared his chest, dipping his stance to match the cat's next to him. He could not help but feel his smile begin to grow.

It was a fleeting smile though, for the deafening hum that escaped from within Prometheus's black mist was devastating. A dark, black cloud shot straight into the air, creating a towering hell of thick mist. Derek's stomach turned over at the thought of the void in all of its glory. Thankfully, this was not the mile-long pillar of darkness from his memory that stood in front of him, but a more subdued vision of despair. Of course, even in its weakened state, the void was still truly something to behold.

The hum solidified in Derek's ears and the clearing itself. He could hear nothing else as its sound pulsed through his skull in waves. Gradually, the mist settled in a swirling tornado around Prometheus's lean body. He stood tall, overlooking everything his eyes fell upon. No words escaped his mouth. No sounds escaped his person. All Derek could hear was the void and the hum.

Prometheus lowered his head, again raising his hands outward. Every creature tensed at the ready. His fingers curled under his hands. With each crackling joint, the ground began to shake. He looked at the first set of squirrels and thrust his palm into the air, sending each tree in their direction flying with it. He lifted his second hand and another set of trees flew forth. The earth split in two. He squashed his hands in front of him, forcing the trees and dirt and earth together, forming them into a solid wrecking ball. Mist shot forth from his arms, wrapping around his new creation as he sprung into the air and swung back and forth, ripping through the forest.

The squirrels jumped and dodged in response, flying acrobatically in groups of four. Each group landed softly on the ground in their own diamond formation, their tails held high to the air. Prometheus was ready. He lifted his mace of earth and stone into the air and threw it as hard as he could at the ground. The earth shattered in response. Prometheus held forth his fingers, pointing from group to group of the gathering squirrels. Bales of fire shot forth from the new openings in the earth toward each formation, but none seemed to hit. Again and again he tried, his face determined like an etched and darkened stone. It was futile. Each stream extinguished in a slight puff of wind as the sky overhead began to darken.

A hundred different shadows speckled the clearing. The low hum of the void's rage began to subdue as a new sound finally broke through. It was not much, but Derek had never been so happy to hear the beating of wings. Overhead, an enormous gathering of birds began to circle. There were so many different shapes and sizes: eagles and owls, falcons and robins, even some Derek did not know. In pairs of their respective species they began to drop while screeching out war cries and plummeting to the earth.

The void roared around Prometheus as he too saw what was approaching. He lifted his hands in a flurry, shooting silver tornados from the ground up towards the falling birds. The birds twisted and shrieked together as they twirled in and out of the tornados like an easy dance they were born to jig. They pulsed past Prometheus in streaks of light and wind, their wake exploding in fires of purple, blue and gold. It was all Prometheus could do to just ward them off. The mist shot forth from his entire being now, blocking and parrying the brilliant flashes of compressed air.

Not to be forgotten, the squirrels appeared directly underneath the floating man. Together they gathered in a perfect circle, surrounding Prometheus from below. Each squirrel was on its hind legs now, snouts and hands rocking back and forth in sync. Lightning formed directly at their center, hissing while it gained in heat and mass until it shot straight up and struck Prometheus from underneath.

With a simple and effortless twist, Prometheus let his body fall just enough to the side so that the lightning would not be a direct hit. As he fell, the black mist solidified like a ball, surrounding him from top to bottom. It twisted in streams of black, clashing again and again against the onslaught of the elements. Dirt, wind, fire; it did not matter. Each was ineffective and each only evaporated into nothingness. The swirling ball of black became a perfect defense against every element the animals could muster. Prometheus settled his center and tucked his legs underneath him.

Then came the howls. Piercing yet deep, the clearing exploded with the sound of battle cries. Wolves in packs of six began to propel themselves from deep within the forest, fangs bared and snarls ready. The earth burst under their paws, lifting to add a bounce to each step. Together they rode on a current of rock and mineral as they bobbed and weaved upwards through blasts of black mist. The first pack to reach Prometheus howled and raised their snouts to the wind. In unison, each wolf turned on his heel and cut directly in the air, angled sharply toward the floating man. They charged like a bushel of arrows, shooting past Prometheus with a high pitched squeal. The mist exploded at their touch in a rage of black fire.

A second ball of mist appeared out of thin air, some ten feet away. It swirled in and of itself, shimmering into existence while Prometheus sat calmly in the middle. Without missing a beat, the wolves launched themselves forward. Like a choreographed dance, the wolf packs would attack and the mist would evaporate and then reappear unscathed. It soon became too much for the mist to handle though, for as soon as the mist vanished, a new pack was already launching at where it would be. Whether by a trick of light or by a catch of the right scent, the wolves were keeping Prometheus on the defensive.

A group of hawks plummeted into the fray, their wings unfurling as one. Prometheus turned, surprised by the new addition. The mist churned, attempting to block the hawks in haste, but it was all for naught. The hawks disbanded and the first pack of wolves came shooting through like a deadly bullet. Time seemed to slow. Derek's breath caught in his throat. It was all he could do to stop from cheering when the decoy worked. The wolves plummeted into the mist, dispersing the all-encompassing defense in a flash of glory. Prometheus grunted and was sent flying to the ground.

When he landed, the animals were ready. More and more poured out of the surrounding forest. Each group sent a different barrage of wind, earth, fire and water towards the falling Prometheus. It was absolute chaos. Rats were popping out of the ground, sending boulders flying like missiles. Birds were descending from the sky in clouds of hail and wind and thunder. Even the wolves were still on the assault, circling their prey as one. What was once a sure victory in Prometheus's favor was quickly crumbling before him. The mist did its best to defend its vessel, but even the impenetrable fortress of twisting black particles could not keep up against the barrage it faced. Prometheus's face began to twist in flashes of rage, anger, disdain and even the slightest hint of fear.

Finally, the last group of animals descended from the forest and into the clearing. One by one they walked in, letting their presence known. A panther led the pack; seven feet in height with a tail curling and twisting into the air. Smooth as velvet and purple as a bruise, the tail must have been twice the size of the panther itself. Next to the panther rolled an old and battered panda bear, engulfing the feline in his shadow. The panda did not even walk. He rolled around in a massive ball, his legs twisted underneath him. Overhead, a withering python slithered out from the treetops. His endless body moved through limbs and leaves as it drooped to the ground. The massive snake must have at least been twenty feet in length. Each scale on his body shone like blood red leather in the sunlight, thick and strong. On his head rode a squirrel so tiny and decrepit that four of them could have fit inside the python's closed mouth. Lastly, an owl landed next to them with feathers every shade of gray, both deep and shallow. He squawked a low and earthy call as he unfurled his gigantic wingspan.

Behind them, a one-eyed wolf appeared with a tall and lean man following beside him. It was the man Derek knew as Mr. Everhart.

"Well, I'll be damned," the cat said, jumping lightly onto Derek's shoulder. His tail wrapped loosely across the boy's arm. "It has been a very, very long time since I have seen the council actually do anything." His eyes twinkled. "How marvelous."

Derek clutched the book to his chest and noted how odd of a trio they must have made.

The fight in front of them raged on. Prometheus was losing the battle and clearly the war. The sacred council of animals surrounded him now in a star like fashion. In harmony, the council members raised a respective appendage into the air; a wing, a paw, a tail. The mist coursed in response, sending its thick black tendrils like whips at each new element. Slowly, the mist began to disperse. The council was too much for it to handle in its weakened state. Inch by blackened inch, the mist was beaten back directly into Prometheus's body as the attack increased in speed and fury. Every element swirled like one until eventually they began to form into a crystallized cage. Prometheus was enraged, the mist fighting until the bitter end. His eyes bulged in shock while he watched his new prison solidify around him into a perfect cube. It shrunk in size and coursed with thunder and ice in its veins.

The council began to walk forward, each member with its head held high in pride. Around them, the other animals settled in the forest and watched in awe while the council took over. With each step and slither, the cage hardened and settled around the man once known as Prometheus. He roared and punched and kicked but the mist only dispersed harmlessly against the forming prison.

The cage crystallized with a simple and underwhelming click. Prometheus was silent. He hunched over, his hands drooping to the ground, before taking a deep breath and calming himself. Then, he stood. His face was yet again a blank slate of nothingness, though his eyes flickered to the ground in curiosity. Derek caught the look, but he knew not what it meant. Prometheus was defeated, cast down yet again. How could he be so calm?

The dust around the cage settled and every being in earshot sighed in a collective agreement. The air was hot and thin, which made it hard to breathe and rough to taste. The animals began to gather themselves in groups, tending to the wounded and rounding up the deceased. The council gathered next to the cage, conversing hurriedly. It was the owl who seemed to do most of the talking. He was not the largest animal of the bunch, but he was certainly the most intimidating. The cat's tail tensed around Derek's arm. Derek looked up at him, curious. The panda bear had just stolen a glance their way. Was the cat actually nervous for once?

"I know what you're thinking," the cat said coldly. "Stop." Derek only smiled in response.

"It is good to see you safe, Derek," a man said over his shoulder. Derek turned on his heel, tensed and responsive. In front of him stood Mr. Everhart, though it was not the same smiling teacher he once knew. Mr. Everhart seemed more refined now, with purpose in his stance. His clothes were tattered, his hair disheveled, but still he managed to give off an air of importance. A lone wolf stood at his side, ever snarling with his last and remaining eye. The cat's tail loosened off of Derek's arm and began to sway back and forth in motion. Derek took a step back.

"What are you doing here?" Derek asked, looking around the clearing. The council was walking towards him now. His heart began to race.

"No need to be alarmed," Mr. Everhart said soothingly. "All your questions will be answered."

"Then start talking. Why are you with the animals?" He began to back up, his mind now racing with the dragon's death on repeat. It flashed again and again in his head, obstructing his vision. "How did Prometheus get here? *What are you doing here?*"

"Calm down, little one," a voice rumbled gently in his ear. The great gray owl landed gently in front of Derek, his gigantic wingspan beating softly. Derek turned again as the council surrounded him. Instantly the pressure released on his mind and his heart slowed. Curious, it was. His brow furrowed and his mind wandered.

He looked at the cage and found Prometheus now staring directly at him.

"Your questions shall be answered shortly," the owl said, his beak clicking as he nodded. "First, we need to know where the dragon is." The council nodded their approval.

Derek's gaze broke from Prometheus. He blinked in indignation. "The dragon died," he said, pointing to where the dragon's carcass lay. "Prometheus shot him in the head right . . . over there." But as Derek looked over the battlefield, the dragon's carcass was nowhere to be found. It had vanished completely, dissipating into thin air.

"Are you sure?" the python hissed. The council looked at Derek nervously.

"Of course I'm sure," Derek snapped. He did not like the snake's tone. "I saw it happen!"

"Now Derek, they are not questioning you," Mr. Everhart said. "They just want to know exactly what happened. I think we all do."

"Prometheus shot the dragon, the dragon died." Derek sighed, throwing up his hands in anger. He looked at Prometheus, sitting in his cage. He shivered as they made eye contact. Why was he still staring at him? "That's it. That's what happened."

"If the great beast died as you claim," the panda bear slurred, rolling onto his hind legs. "Then where are the remains?" He huffed in laughter, his black and while jowls jiggling along. "Dead things do not just disappear."

"I don't know how it works," Derek said, exasperated. "Have any of you ever seen a dragon die?"

"Yes, I have," the great owl said, silencing the group. "And if the boy says the dragon died, then the dragon died." He lifted his great wings into the air, trying to help calm the group's nerves. "If so, we do not have very much time at all. We must prepare ourselves for the beginning of the next cycle. These births are usually a messy, messy thing. Who knows what could happen!" The owl scanned the clearing, clicking his beak together rapidly. "Now, where is—"

In a violent crack and in one swooping motion, the earth underneath began to twist and grumble. Everything on legs fell over in an instant. The birds not quick enough to take flight fell from the trees. Derek clutched the book. The cat was screaming something at him now but he could not hear. His head was filled with a low and ominous buzzing. The earth moved again, knocking him on his back. He rolled over and found himself looking straight into a volcanic pit of earth as it split from its very roots. He rolled again, trying to keep his wits about him, to find solid ground. Fire shot up from deep within the breaking earth, singeing his hair.

Just as Derek forced himself onto his knees, a groaning sound smashed him in the face, though he could not tell if it was the sound or the force of wind that sent him reeling. Lava spewed like fountains all around. What now? What could be attacking? He forced himself to look to the source of the explosion and his heart caught in his throat. This was no attack; the gigantic mountain looming overhead was now splitting in two before his very eyes. From deep within, the mountain began to crumble. Derek yelled to the cat, attempting to be heard over the chaos, but there was little need. The cat was already sprawled in front of him, fangs bared and tail swaying frantically. He did not know exactly what was happening, but every time the lava came at them, it bounced harmlessly away. The cat was keeping them safe.

The mountain collapsed quicker than Derek would have thought, the lumbering beast of rock and boulder crumbling frailly into a pile of rubble. He shielded his face from the dust cloud that came spewing forth, but again the cat seemed to protect them from all danger. He clutched the book to his chest and watched the world collapse around him.

A single, deep chuckle consumed Derek's mind. The laugh trembled down his spine, crackling to the very core of his being. The cat looked up in horror, his every hair raised on end.

"Impossible!" the great gray owl shouted, but Derek knew better. Nothing could be impossible to one who destroys hope. The dust cleared as a gigantic bale of black and twisting smoke shot forth into the sky like a raging tornado. Derek forced himself to follow the tornado's coursing form to its base, knowing already what he would find there.

The crystallized cage sat on its side, cracked and burning beneath the sudden devastation of the earth.

"I AM THAT WHICH CANNOT BE CAGED."

Each animal of the council turned toward the tornado of mist, trying to get up, to stand under the weight of the void's pressure. It was useless. Thick and blackened tendrils of smoke shot out in every direction, wrapping each of the council members within its grasp.

"THAT WHICH CANNOT BE HELD."

Every creature in the area watched in horror as the void began to fill itself within each of the council members. The council members coughed and sputtered, their bodies filling with the mist. Derek watched in agony. If there were screams or cries of anguish, they could not be heard over the pounding voice rattling through his skull.

"I AM CREATION AND DESTRUCTION. THAT WHICH EXISTS BEFORE AND BEYOND THE AGES."

The void released the majestic animals in a flurry, throwing each to the ground with a sickening thud. Derek choked back the tears, this time ready for the overwhelming feeling of despair that began to swell inside of him. He looked to Mr. Everhart, surprised to find him pressed against the ground on one knee, staring defiantly in the black tornado's direction. The one-eyed wolf stood beside him, each leg shaking to keep his stance. Mr. Everhart screamed something then, but it was lost to the wind.

"THIS AGE HAS LASTED FAR BEYOND ITS OWN EXISTENCE."

The middle of the tornado began to part, just enough to reveal Prometheus's stoic face and blackened eyes. He looked down amongst the rabble below him, completely unimpressed.

"REMEMBER YOU ARE NOTHING AS IT ENDS BEFORE YOU."

Prometheus disappeared then, the black tornado enveloping him once again. It shot like a rocket into the sky. Every cloud it touched shuddered into an explosion of thunder and lightning, wavering like it had just been defiled. Derek did not know where the void was headed, but he was glad to see it disappear. It left only the sound of thunder and crackling lightning in its wake as it faded off into the distance.

Gradually, the clearing started to stir. Once a beautiful patchwork of grass surrounded by age-old trees, it was now torn apart at the roots in every way imaginable. The earth was ripped and uneven. The trees were scattered for what seemed like half a mile, strewn about carelessly. Even the leftover grass was withered and black from the random bits of fire and lightning that had been thrown at it.

However, what stood out the most was the now crumbled mountain before them.

The animals began to make their way to the crumpled bodies of the council members, with Mr. Everhart and the one-eyed wolf leading the way. He crouched over the great owl and the wolf whispered something solemnly. They helped the owl sit up. One by one, the council members followed. The panda sat forward, his face a state of complete shock. The panther sat back on her hind legs, not wanting to be touched. Her long tail slashed the air. She roared then in a type of anguish that Derek did not understand. It seemed to him that the council members were each alive and well. Derek breathed a sigh of relief.

The cat sighed, too, but it was the furthest thing from relief. "You think that they're completely unscathed, don't you?" the cat said, sitting on his hind legs. Derek half expected the cat to begin licking a paw as he normally would, but the cat just sat and stared in the council's direction.

Derek nodded slowly. None of the animals seemed happy, even to be alive. His brow darkened.

"They're not." The cat only shook his head then, half in disgust and half in determination. He looked at Derek, his bright golden eyes piercing through him. "That thing, that darkness . . ." The cat sniffed the air as if tasting for something. He nodded to himself solemnly. "It took away their understanding, Derek."

Derek let the words sink in. "You mean, their magic?"

"Yes, their *magic*," the cat nodded, "though I would not be so bold as to call it that to their faces." Complete and utter doom was now splashed across the face of each member. The panther roared again, her teeth gnashing in the air.

"Imagine your sense of touch, of taste, of sight and hearing," the cat continued amid the roars. "Now, imagine each of them being completely shut off to you in an instant. You can still feel them, though. Your brain still remembers the smell of a cascading rain, the sound of a pebble rolling down a hill, but it now knows you'll never have those things again."

"How do you know?" Derek asked.

"It is the worst part of what happens when I die." With that, the cat began to lick his paw.

Derek let the silence hang in the air. Slowly, the animals gathered themselves and began yet again to tend to their dead and wounded. The council members that had regained their composure, mainly the great owl and the ancient tiny squirrel, lead their groups into organized cleanup crews. The panda bear sat paralyzed, staring at the ground in utter dismay. He did not cry, he did not scream, he barely even flinched while other animals gathered around him. Instead, he just sat and stared at the ground. When the python finally gained his composure, he slithered away into the forest without a word. By then, the panther was long gone.

"I think your book is trying to talk to you," the cat said. Derek had almost completely forgotten about the book still clutched tightly in his arms. He looked down to find it pulsating madly, its glow burning white hot. He opened it and stared into its glowing depths, smiling as he felt the small weight of a girl's hand land softly on his shoulder.

"We don't have much time, Derek," Tella said in his ear.

"Tella, I'm so sorry!" he blurted out. The tears began to gather in his eyes as he turned around. "Caelus, all of it, it's all my fault—"

Tella silenced him with a single hug. He shivered under its precious weight, letting it sink in. "What's done is done," she whispered softly in his ear. "You are not to blame, child." She leaned back and smiled at Derek. He could not help but smile back.

"For now, we have things we must accomplish," Tella said finitely. She looked at the cat, unable to mask her contempt. "You can sustain this, correct?" Her tone was icy, but the cat just nodded in response. He flicked his tail, lifting the book into the air inside a small, blue flame. The book seemed to devour the flame then, gobbling up its essence. The light began to pour from within, cascading Tella's image unto the world.

Tella checked herself and nodded her approval. "Good," she said, steadying herself lightly. "This will have to do until the dragon learns how."

"Dragon?" Derek said, getting to his feet. He wiped the remaining tears back. "But . . . Caelus died."

Tella flinched at the words, and Derek wished instantly that he could have taken them back. She did not scold his brashness, though. "Yes, he did," she said, letting her face soften. Her eyes flicked to the cat then in a brief moment of rage, but it was the only sign of emotion she let out. "But we will deal with those responsible for this in due time."

"How gracious of you," the cat muttered, rolling his eyes.

"For now, the world still turns and the cycle must continue." Tella nodded to herself in thought. "It is a bit premature, but I think together we can all accomplish this." Tella turned around on her heel, walking decisively toward where the mountain once stood.

"Uh, we?" Derek turned to the cat. "Did she say we?"

"Yes," the cat said coolly, eyes weighing the situation. "I do believe she did."

"Yes, I do believe I did." Tella stood there, her hands on her hips. She cocked an eyebrow and waited patiently for them to follow.

Yet another roar ripped through the clearing then. Every animal tensed and took a defensive stance. All eyes were cast upon the sky, knowing surely what was to come. Tella laughed to herself and turned on her heel. "Come," she said, walking toward the crumbled mountain. "It is time."

The roar ripped through the air again, sparking every creature's curiosity. Derek followed in step. After a moment, he realized that the animals had begun to follow behind them. Together, they scaled the rocks and rubble of the crumbled mountain toward the growing sound of bellowing. Off in the distance, a black puff of smoke raised into the air, accompanied with yet another cry. Over and over, the sound of the roar broke the sky. Over and over, a brand new puff of smoke raised into the air with it, until eventually the smoke turned into a tiny stream of fire. Derek's heart began to race. Could it be? Quickly, he rounded the last boulder and came down upon what must have been the center of the mountain. Directly in front of him, a single egg lay cracked in half.

On top of that egg, a shimmering charcoal colored dragon barely the size of Derek's forearm sat on her haunches. She flexed her tiny wings and roared again and again. Derek smiled despite himself. The roar was neither in anger nor in angst, but more akin to the sound of a chuckle. Derek watched the dragon roll around on the ground. Her deep silver scales glistened and shined like newborn ash in the sunlight. The dragon stopped, growing silent. She sniffed in the air before spouting one last stream of fire and twisting her head around towards them. The baby dragon stared at the creatures now staring at her.

Tella led the group, walking her way to the hatchling. "Hello there, friend," she said, kneeling beside her. "Do you know me?"

The dragon stared into her eyes and nodded, her own eyes a glistening dark purple. Tella smiled. In response, the dragon coughed and flicked out her tongue, shooting a brief bit of smoke into Tella's face before taking off into the air.

Tella recoiled indignantly. "How rude!" she huffed, folding her arms.

"Oh, I like this one already," the cat chuckled to himself.

The dragon joined in the cat's laughter, chuckling deep within her own throat. She circled overhead, looping and twirling through the air, before she caught a scent she seemed to like dearly. She roared in elation, sending up three puffs of fire as if unable to control herself. She turned, twisting her slender silver body around in mid air and dove directly toward Derek. Derek did not even have a chance to move before the dragon had landed safely on his shoulder. He stared at her, wondering how something so large could feel so light. To be sure, the dragon would certainly grow much bigger over time, but for now she rested lightly across his shoulders. The dragon caught his eye and chuckled. She pressed her snout against his neck and nestled playfully. Derek looked up and found every single eye staring at him then. He looked at the cat and did the only thing he could think of.

Derek laughed.

The cat turned to Tella with a smile. "It seems that after ages with just your company, the dragon race is happy for some new companionship." A single eyebrow rose on Tella's face. It was the only discernible bit of emotion in an otherwise icy stare.

"Uh, hi there," Derek said to the creature attempting to cuddle with him.

"I think he likes you," the cat said with a slight smile.

"She," Derek said knowingly. He blinked. How on earth did he know that? He looked at the dragon, shocked by his own sudden knowledge. Their eyes met again and instantly they giggled together. He could not explain it, though he was not sure he cared to. They laughed again. It was all so overwhelming. In that moment, he knew the dragon as if she were an extension of his own being, of his own mind. He felt his cheeks flush as he lost himself in the dragon's purple gaze. The dragon nodded. She too knew every single particle of his being. Derek felt completely naked.

"Well, I'll be damned," the cat said, breaking Derek's concentration. "I think they just bonded."

Immediately, Derek's head whipped around to the dragon. She nodded. He felt his cheeks flush again in embarrassment. The dragon chuckled in response. Derek could tell she had felt it, too. Derek could also tell that she found it extremely amusing.

"Do not spout nonsense, cat," the great gray owl said. He landed softly behind them, a group of smaller owls behind him in formation. He clicked his beak in thought, bowing to Tella. The other owls followed suit. "It has been too long, my lady."

Tella nodded in recognition, though her concentration was clearly on Derek and his dark silver dragon.

The cat looked surprised. "You two know each other?" he asked in his most sincere voice. Derek could not help but smile at that.

"We met a long time ago, when I was made leader of this council," Abraham said, puffing out his chest proudly. "I was led to her and her dragon counterpart to learn the imperative nature of their bond." Abraham nodded lightly. The other owls nodded in unison. "Together, they told me a grand tale of how their sacrifice kept the world spinning, though they were very light on the details." Abraham's head cocked slightly, his beak clicking as he gathered his thoughts. "When this man was thrust into our captivity," Abraham said, pointing to Mr. Everhart, "he began to talk of a magic book that both he and his old friend had spoken of. Instantly, I knew something was amiss." Tella met Abraham's eyes then, both staring with an icy glare. "Only now do I begin to understand exactly what it was that had broken the world."

"You were given the information you needed and nothing more," Tella said without hesitation.

The one-eyed wolf stepped forward, his teeth bared in a growl. "But if the council had known more, maybe this entire situation could have been avoided!" The surrounding animals began to murmur their agreement. The wolf flashed his teeth in disgust.

Tella's eyes were slits, her voice cold and without feeling. "You were given the information you needed and nothing more," she said in defiance. "We could not risk any creature getting curious." She did not exactly look at the cat then, but the intent was more than enough. "We thought we had it under control. We were wrong." She let the words hang in the air.

"Does it really matter now?" Derek blurted out. Every head turned in his direction. He shrugged. "I mean, Prometheus, or whatever that thing is, is out there right now, right? Isn't that the biggest concern?" As he let the question ring true, he could feel the burst of pride welling up inside the dragon. He could not help but blush again.

"It seems the boy is the one with the most sense," the cat said, hopping his way over to Derek. "Indeed, what are we going to do about it? It did promise quite profusely to end the age, you know." The cat's tail flicked coolly. "It seems that is quite the pressing matter."

"But we are powerless against it!" the one-eyed wolf growled again.

"Quinn is right," Mr. Everhart said, stepping forward. "Obviously whatever has possessed my old friend is clearly not in the mood to negotiate, nor is it weak. It seemed to me that even at our best it still overwhelmed us." Mr. Everhart looked to Abraham then, a sudden sadness washing over his face.

Quinn growled deep within his throat. His single eye looked to the ground in despair. "Then we are hopeless." The words hit like a weight.

"There is a way," Tella said, turning her attention toward Derek and the baby dragon. Every eye followed her gaze.

The cat smiled to Abraham smugly. "I told you they had bonded."

"Impossible!" Abraham hooted. "It is forbidden!"

"Only because I forbid it in the first place," Tella answered, her tone silencing all who heard. "It was to keep us from repeating our mistakes." Tella sighed in remission. "But, either the traps each dragon and I set to protect us grew weaker over the eons or it seems there is a creature or two out there who has done something terrible to gain knowledge outside of my own understanding."

Every eye turned to the cat. His eyebrows raised in curiosity. "I haven't the slightest idea of what you are you implying."

"Be that as it may," Tella continued, returning her focus to Derek and the baby dragon, "I fear we are going to need the both of them." She nodded to Abraham, offering herself a slight smile. "I just pray they can learn to harness their bond in time."

"Wow, wait, hold on—what?" Derek said as the information began to process. "You mean, I mean, I hope you don't mean—I'm a kid! You can't mean—"

"Yes," the great owl said. He patted Derek on the back and bobbed his majestic head. "You're going to have to save the world, boy."

Derek could feel his heart pounding within his chest. Or was that the dragon's heart? He could not tell. He felt the dragon's tail tighten around his arm. His heart slowed while an odd sense of peace set in. He breathed deeply, allowing the strange stillness to wash over him. He looked at the dragon, already knowing the twinkle that would be in her eyes.

"To put it bluntly, yes," Tella said. "The second this dragon chose you, are you doomed to its friendship." A small hint of yearning gleamed within her eyes. "It seems we must put our trust in you."

Derek nodded slowly, his eyes trained on the dragon. It was an odd sort of knowing that had set in, but for whatever reason the task at hand did not seem so daunting. Yes, the beast that had been unleashed was menacing and absolutely unbending, but as he peered into the dragon's eyes, he knew the truth of the issue. It did not matter how absolutely absurd it seemed, it just mattered that Derek could feel it was possible. Together, they could change the world. The dragon nodded in response. Derek could not help but smile.

His brow furrowed. A thought clicked from deep within his mind. "What about my family?" he asked, turning to the cat. "What will happen to them?"

Every eye turned in tandem on the cat. He shrugged. "I guess they'll be fine as long as Prometheus doesn't target them."

"So they'll just think I'm missing?" Derek's voice was barely a whisper. "Like I just abandoned them and that's it?"

"Yes," the cat nodded slowly, weighing Derek in his own gaze. Derek let the word hang in the air, deciding on his next course of action. The dragon flicked a wing in response, already knowing exactly what he was thinking. He breathed deeply and readied himself.

"Can you make them forget me?" Derek let the silence fall over all who heard the question. "Can you make it like I never existed to them? I don't want them to worry." He was surprised at how easy the question was. After all that had happened though, what choice did he have?

"Yes, Derek," said the cat quietly. "I can make them forget you."

The words stood still in the air, no one creature wanting to take up the heavy mantle. As always, Tella nodded to herself. "Then, if that's settled . . ." She raised her arms to her side and began to float into the air. Her image grew in size until it filled up the sky enough for all to see.

"I'm not going to lie to you," her voice boomed over the crowd of animals. "What has been unleashed upon this world once stood as the greatest threat I have ever seen. I know it as a void. It is complete and absolute destruction. We do not know its origin, we do not know its purpose, but what we do know is that the damage it can cause is extraordinary." She gestured to the clearing behind them and the crumbled mountain they now stood upon. "This is but a fraction of its power. In all honesty, I do not think we can handle the void if it were to ever gain even half of that power back." She breathed deeply, letting the information sink in. "But, we are all still standing and still breathing, and thus we are not without hope." Every eye turned to Derek and the dragon as she pointed to him. "Together, I believe we stand a chance."

Tella's image shimmered down to her normal self, letting her words hang in her place. Lightly, she walked over to Derek and the dragon and placed a hand on the dragon's head. She caressed the newborn creature with a sullen smile and met Derek's eye.

"Are you ready, Derek?" Tella asked plainly.

"Hell no," he blurted out, surprising even himself. The dragon chuckled on his shoulder.

"Well, get ready," the cat said with a laugh. "I don't think you have a choice."

Quinn growled. "The cat is right about that."

Mr. Everhart turned to Tella, his face beaming with pride. "Just tell us what we must do." Every animal in earshot nodded in agreement.

"First," Tella said all too quickly, "We must teach them how to cultivate their bond." She turned to Derek then, her face beaming with optimism.

"And how on earth can we do that?" the great owl boomed, ruffling his feathers. "No creature has bonded since the dawn of our recognition." The great owl puffed up his chest. "Can you do it?"

"No, I cannot," Tella shook her head solemnly. "I do not exist in the way you do, I am not living. I cannot teach them anything."

"Then we are lost!" Abraham said, throwing up his wings in despair.

"No," Tella smiled. "We just need a very, very old friend. Someone that the ages have all but forgotten." Derek gasped, a single image flashing in his head. He looked at the dragon, knowing it was she who had given him the answer. She only nodded in response, her deep and now violet eyes glinting as they caught the sunlight.

Tella smiled at the both of them. "She told you then?"

"Yeah," Derek said bewildered. "How did she do that?"

"The dragons are a connected race," Tella said, her eyes glossing over in thought. "All knowledge is passed between them and thus nothing is forgotten." The dragon smiled knowingly. Derek felt his chest swell up in a sudden sense of pride. It was the first emotion they had shared together.

"Mind letting us in on the secret?" the cat asked, attempting to lick his paw indifferently, but failing.

Derek smirked. "You can't stand that I know something and you don't." The dragon blew a little puff of smoke in agreement.

"Cute," the cat said sarcastically. "I just think the whole world ending thing is a bit more pressing."

Derek scanned the animal kingdom now watching his every move. He looked to the broken trees and torn ground before the mountain, to the book floating above them. He looked to Mr. Everhart, to the cat and to the remainder of the animal council. Lastly, he looked to the dragon nestling on his shoulder. There she sat, always peering into his very soul. He could not describe his feelings for her in any words he had known, but the connection they shared offered little need to do so. He knew what must be done.

He looked to Tella and shrugged. "Well, where do we find them?" he asked.

Tella's eyes glistened against the dragon's silvery scales. "She knows," smiling her approval to the dragon.

Derek's breath caught in his chest as the knowledge filled his entire being. "Oh," he breathed, his mind flooding with new information. He caught his breath and looked to his new friend. "Well then," he began with a smirk. "Let's get going, shall we?"

EPILOGUE

On a desolate island a thousand miles from any discernible coast, thought or living being, the sun cracked the sky in two as it conquered the horizon. The island itself was unassuming, barely a floating plot of land carved out from centuries of earthquakes and other unlucky omens. The beaches were white and blinding in the sunlight and not a single footstep could be found along its flowing shores of black and crackling boulders. The island lounged lazily in the sea, continuously untouched by man or beast. Peaceful and alone it sat, under countless blue horizons and endlessly lonesome clouds.

Today though, the horizon was different. Today it was dark and menacing, almost maroon in color and black in nature. Every cloud in sight was bunched together across the ocean in a single and ominous point at the sky's edge.

For most who would see the spectacle that morning, it would be but an anomaly, just a singular striking picture of nothing more than an atmospheric build up and release of molecular tension. The clouds themselves would be put into pictures and paintings, maybe even chatted about over meandering mornings worldwide, but in the end the skyline would be forgotten just like the countless ones before it. In the end, it would be but a trivial beauty and nothing more.

In the middle of the island, a single black boulder cracked in half, revealing a small tunnel leading deep within the earth. A single man arose from the tunnel, shielding his eyes as they caught the sunlight for the first time in a millennium. The morning air brushed lightly against his open skin, sending shivers throughout his body. He looked to the horizon in horror and cursed underneath his breath.

He had been right. He had felt its return, the tingling sensation in his arm that was no more. His stomach churned in disgust. Bile filled his throat. He spat and cursed whatever wretched soul had unleashed the void again. Hoping that he was wrong was meaningless. Damn it all, but the feeling in his gut had been right.

He broke through the tree line of the desolate island so far from any human's recollection and his stomach churned at the sight of the gathering horizon. The wind whipped at his hair, but he could not be bothered by it. Again, he shuddered, though he did not think it was because of the cold. It had been so long since he had allowed himself to see the sunrise, he had truly hoped that he would see it again under different circumstances.

A low and melodic sigh caught his ear as his old friend began to pace the beach behind him. "It was only a matter of time, wasn't it?" The voice was soft but the words were heavier than the world could know.

The man nodded in response, staring down the sunrise with purpose. He smiled, remembering the days when they were both so young and naïve. Back then things were easier. How long ago was that age before the void existed, before all he knew was torn asunder? Again he cursed under his breath.

"It really was," he answered somberly. He stretched out his only arm, petting the eight feet of black and sleek fur now standing beside him. The fox looked at him then, all three of his tails swaying lightly in the breeze. They met each other's eyes in silence: both pairs were a perfect shade of silver. No pupils, no whites, just pure and unadulterated gray.

The fox sighed, shaking his head in worry. "Alexander, I don't think this world is ready." He looked out over the horizon, watching as the sky grew darker and darker in the distance before turning back to his old friend for an answer.

Alexander scratched his stump of an arm methodically. It was an old habit to be sure, but it was one he could never quite break. He thought of Aden's question and hesitated. He did not want to admit it specifically, but deep down he knew his old friend was right.

He just prayed they were both wrong.

ABOUT THE AUTHOR

In a quiet town, in a quiet village, a boy was born. This boy grew up obsessed with Pokemon, guitars and all things fantasy. Samuel Tucker Young is a mid-twenties dork with a passion for writing and an even greater desire to listen.

Made in the USA
San Bernardino, CA
10 August 2014